Midlands

Edited by Lynsey Hawkins

Disclaimer

Young Writers has maintained every effort
to publish stories that will not cause offence.

Any stories, events or activities relating to individuals
should be read as fictional pieces and not construed
as real-life character portrayal.

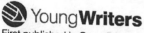 Young**Writers**

First published in Great Britain in 2004 by:
Young Writers
Remus House
Coltsfoot Drive
Peterborough
PE2 9JX
Telephone: 01733 890066
Website: www.youngwriters.co.uk

SB ISBN 1 84460 618 X

Foreword

Young Writers was established in 1991 and has been passionately devoted to the promotion of reading and writing in children and young adults ever since. The quest continues today. *Young Writers* remains as committed to engendering the fostering of burgeoning poetic and literary talent as ever.

This year, *Young Writers* are happy to present a dynamic and entertaining new selection of the best creative writing from a talented and diverse cross-section of some of the most accomplished primary school writers around. Entrants were presented with three inspirational and challenging themes.

'Mini Sagas' set pupils the challenge of writing a story in 50 words or less. This style of story telling required considerable thought and effort to create a complete story with such a strict word limit.

'A Day In The Life Of . . .' offered pupils the chance to depict twenty-four hours in the lives of literally anyone they could imagine. A hugely imaginative wealth of entries were received encompassing days in the lives of everyone from the top media celebrities to historical figures like Henry VIII or a typical soldier from the First World War.

Finally 'Short Stories' offered the authors free reign with their writing style and subject matter. All themes encouraged the writer to open and explore their minds as they used their imagination to produce the following selection.

All Write! Midlands is ultimately a collection we feel sure you will love, featuring as it does the work of the best young authors writing today. We hope you enjoy the work included and will continue to return to *All Write! Midlands* time and time again in the years to come.

Contents

Jade Morris (11) 37
Alison Roberts (11) 38
Lucinda Roberts (11) 39
Gary Jones (10) 40
Andy Rowbottom (10) 41
Roseanne Gregory (11) 42
Sam Farrington (11) 43
Bryony Marlow-Spalding (10) 44

Ettington CE Primary School, Ettington

Oliver Rose (10) 45
Megan Stanley (9) 46
Nathan Geekie (9) 47
Robert Lilley (11) 48
Joseph Lucas (10) 49
Ashleigh Cotton (11) 50
Laura Woodfield (10) 51
Charlotte Holmes (9) 52
Bethan Payne (10) 53
Barnaby Galiffe (8) 54
Gemma Griffin (8) 55
Megan Bradshaw (9) 56
Ellie Rathkey (8) 57
Alexander Marney (9) 58
Hannah Hope (8) 59
Megan Barnwell (8) 60
Daniel Regan (8) 61
Sophie Holmes (8) 62
Jonathan Vestentoft (9) 63
Daniel Hope (9) 64
Georgina Brooks (9) 65
Frances Goss (9) 66
Harry Mace-Hartley (9) 67
Alice Herring (9) 68
Megan Stanley (9) 69
Ben Allen (9) 70
Ben Plant (9) 71
Lucy Allen (9) 72
Sasha Drake (7) 73
Phoebe Leathart (9) 74

Fairway JI School, Kings Norton

Dani Szucs	75
Shannon Reilly (9)	76
Hope Douglas	77
Tori Spittle	78
Nikisha Talbot (11)	79
Jessica Evans	80
Charlotte Jenkins (11)	81
Danielle Bourne (11)	82
Jessica Perrin (11)	83
Bhavana Ghai	84

Langmoor Primary School, Oadby

Rose Piggott-Smith (8)	85
Felicity Roles (9)	86
Daljinder Johal (9)	87
Emily Bexon (9)	88
Andrew Harris (9)	89
Danielle Leadbitter (9)	90
Harriet Hewitt (9)	91
Holly Ilott (9)	92
Ravine Walker (9)	93
Emma Willson (9)	94
Reece Ridgway (9)	95
Luke Phillips (9)	96

Longden CE Primary School, Shrewsbury

Kate Nixon (10)	97
Louise Smith Ellis (10)	98
Laura Wallen (11)	99
Lucy Lewis (10)	100
Lucy Hickson (10)	101
Maddy Cartwright (11)	102
Jennifer Morgan (10)	103
Sam Rintoul (10)	104
Georgina Davies (10)	105
Cerian Abbott (10)	106
Becky Griffiths (11)	107
Stephen Raymond (11)	108
Josie Murtha (10)	109

Emily Cox (11)   110
Laura Price (9)   111

Moorgate Primary School, Tamworth
Karanjeet Dhesi (11)   112
Ben Pickering (9)   113
Charlotte Williamson (11)   114
Lauren Sutherland (11)   115
Jade Soady-Jones (10)   116
Jacob Robertson (9)   117
Mackenzie Ingley (11)   118
Wally Chapman (10)   119
Harriett Keirle (10)   120
Michael Hulme (9)   121
Stefan Hunt (10)   122
Bradley Dukes (10)   123
George Sayce (11)   124
Abi Stephens (10)   125
Simon Dainter (10)   126
Meghan Owen (10)   127
Paul Cotton (10)   128
Tanya Lewis (10)   129
Essam Aljaedy (11)   130
Laura Wesley (11)   131
Sarah Guise (10)   132
Stacey Latchford (11)   133

Northleigh CE Primary School, Malvern
Sophie Dawson (10)   134
Mary Fleming (10)   135
Jasmine Mayo (10)   136
Emma Knowles (10)   137
Caryn Bristow (11)   138
Dominic Lane (11)   139
Jared Maxfield (10)   140
Eric Carlen (10)   141
Amelia Arnold (10)   142
Rowan Whitehouse (9)   143
Amy Straughan (9)   144
Jake Stromqvist (8)   145
Alexandra Smith (9)   146

Willows Primary School, Lichfield

Robert Rhodes (10)   231
Jamie Lees (10)   232
Gary Brown (10)   233
Steven Bayliss (10)   234
Rebecca Johnson-Tiso (10)   235
David Smallman (10)   236
Daniel Jewell (9)   237
Aston Blackwell (10)   238
Alex Foyle (10)   239
James Meakin (9)   240
Rachel Wood (10)   241
Megan Shenton (10)   242
Michelle Wilcox (10)   243
Thomas McCaffrey (10)   244
Ryan Poxon (10)   245
Polly Bourne (10)   246
George Makin (10)   247
Ben Cunningham (10)   248
Maria Sammons (10)   249
Sean Wood (9)   250
Sophie Davies (9)   251
Hannah Frazer-Morris (10)   252

The Creative Writing

The Beast Of The Night

I wake to heavy, wet breathing on my face. Rough hands pushing, shaking me to the floor. What could this beast be doing in my room? In circles he chased me round and round. I finally reach the light switch; there stands my worst nightmare my . . . snot-nosed . . . teenage . . . brother.

Zane Burkmar (9)

The True Story Of The Troll And The Grotty Billy Goat's Gruff

It was a scorching hot day, I was just going to doze off when, clip-clop, clip-clop. It was those wretched goats again. I got up and pleaded them to use another bridge. 'Please, please use another bridge,' I moaned.

'No!' said the wretched Billy Goats Gruff.

'You are being unreasonable,' I said. The goats ignored me completely, it was like they were in their own little world.

The next day they came at me stamping like a herd of elephants. They started to knock down my bridge. I got my slingshot out and stones and fired them at the goats. I was about to start to grizzle but suddenly I had the most brilliant idea. I was going to put my bridge further down the stream and put a new one where mine was.

The next morning I awoke to the sound of the alarm clock at 8 o'clock. But the strange thing was that I was expecting to wake up to the sound of the Billy Goats Gruff. I popped my head over the bridge. It was extraordinary. They were using another bridge. I trotted along to the goats and said, 'Thank you so much for using a different bridge.'

Tom Young (9)
Bronington Primary School, Whitchurch

The Red-Headed League

Late at night Holmes and I were waiting in the cellar.
    'Have you remembered the gun?' Holmes whispered to me.
    'Yes,' I replied.
    The lantern was very dim. The clock chimed twelve times. Tip-tap.
    'What's that?' I asked.
    'I don't know,' replied Holmes.
    By this time the lantern wasn't working, but you know Holmes, he's got amazing eyesight - he eats loads of carrots.
    'Ah Mr Duncan Ross,' shouted Holmes.
    'Uh-oh, I'm in deep trouble,' moaned Ross.
    'Yes,' replied Holmes. 'Show us the tunnel,' Holmes ordered.
    'Yes Sir.' Then Ross ran back up the stairs.
    'After him,' shouted Holmes.
    I got my gun out and tried to shoot Ross. We followed him to the train station, he jumped on and so did we. The train was going to the other side of London. I had another shot. It still missed. When we reached the other side of London, Ross tripped on his lace.
    'Shoot!' shouted Holmes.
    Bang! Guess what? It missed. By this time he was off again. He fell again! But this time it was on a banana skin. This time we caught him.
    'Tell us why you are trying to trick us?' I said.
    'I wanted more money,' he replied.
    A policeman came running over. 'Hello, hello, hello, what do we have here?'
    'Well Ross was trying to steal from the bank.'
    'Well you are going to jail for many years my friend!'

A couple of hours later we got back home.
    'I knew it was Ross all along because of his muddy knees when he was at the pawn shop,' Holmes explained.

Edward Muldowney (10)
Bronington Primary School, Whitchurch

The True Story Of The Troll And The Billy Goats

Those blasted goats. Trip-trop-trap-trip. All I want is some shut eye. Their stupid twinkly tails flapping about. Merrily they skip on so stupidly.

'Go away, I need some shut eye!' Oh here they come again. 'Go away.'

'What?' said the goats and off they went.

See what I mean? One day I will kill those pesky goats. Yawn. Good day. 'Ouch!' Those goats are throwing rocks at me - I need to sleep so I can ride the coal mines. 'Go away or I will kill you! I will get out my best slingshot!' I will get my most painful rocks out. They will never survive to see another day. Oh, I'm starting to sound like the Prime Minister! Here they come! *Hit, hit, hit!*

Alex Pullen (9)
Bronington Primary School, Whitchurch

Ryan In The World Cup Final

15th April 2010

Fifteenth April, Ryan Walters' sixteenth birthday. Today he was signing for Arsenal under eighteens for a three year contract. He was very excited.

22nd April 2010

Ryan's first game on the starting line-up. He started on the right defence wing. At half-time the score was 1-0 to Spurs. Arsenal were all over them really. Ryan got moved up into right midfield. At full-time the score was 2-1 thanks to a diving header from a corner, scored by Ryan. The other goal was a cracking bender. On that day Ryan got spotted for England under twenty-ones.

29th April 2010

Ryan had played two games for England by now. He scored in one against Spain and they won 1-0. Today he got picked to go to the World Cup, not for under twenty-ones but for the main team!

30th June 2010

The World Cup flew and now it was the day of the World Cup final. Ryan had been on the bench for most of the tournament but he had had about seven appearances and had scored three times - once against Brazil, which knocked them out, and twice against Romania. Today he was starting. At half-time the score was 1-1 and Wayne Rooney had scored. The second half was a clincher. France were all over them. It went onto silver goal. England had a corner. The ball came out on the volley and he buried it in the top corner. Ryan was a hero!

Ryan Walters (10)
Bronington Primary School, Whitchurch

It's Just A Dream

'*Wwwooff!*'

It sounded like a dog. I looked out of my window and saw a black figure going into the forest across the road. I fell back to sleep.

Knock, knock!

I woke up. It was the door, I was too scared to get out of bed. *Bang!* the door fell down. It was a man, he had sharp teeth and very hairy arms.

'Help me,' he said. 'I'm being hunted by wolves.'

'What's your name?' I asked.

'Max, he replied.

I opened the curtains and Max started turning into ananimal, he started getting really hairy and his face was changing.

'You're a dog,' I said.

'Hhhoowwll.'

'They're coming,' said Max.

I picked up my torch and hid under my cover. I could hear something sniffing my cover. The wolf's breath smelt very, very bad. I could not help it, I had to shout, 'Get yourself some Tic Tacs!'

'Guy, Guy, get up, you're late for school!' said Mum.

It was just a dream!

Guy Davies (10)
Bronington Primary School, Whitchurch

The True Story

One hot day the troll fell asleep. *Trip-trap, trip-trap.* 'Oh that blasted goat on my bridge again waking me up. I have told him that I have to sleep in the day because in the night I work as a miner, that is why I am so mucky.'

He jumped up and scared the grotty goat. He was called 'Doesn't Listen To Trolls'! He jumped in the river and swam away.

'That blasted goat. I will kill him if he goes on my bridge again.' I fell back asleep.

Trip-trap, trip-trap. The troll got a stone, he jumped up and threw the stone at the goat and he was dead. Now he can get some sleep at last.

Daniel Watson (9)
Bronington Primary School, Whitchurch

The Strange Object

One summer afternoon Sam, Chloe, Ben (the dog) and I were playing on the beach when we discovered the body of a lady floating in a rock pool. We saw she was our good friend Helena. We decided to find out what had happened so we began to search the beach.

Suddenly Ben barked - he had found a gun.

'I think Peter has a gun,' Sam whispered.

I said, 'Chloe phone the police and tell them about Helena. Sam, you come with Ben and me. We're going to Peter's house.'

Chloe raced to the telephone box while Sam, Ben and I rushed to find Peter.

Sam hammered on Peter's door.

Peter answered and said, 'Hello, what do you want?'

'We need to talk to you,' said Sam.

'You'd better come in then,' muttered Peter.

We entered nervously, hoping the police were on the way.

'Peter, we have some terrible news, Helena is dead,' I said.

'And we think you know something about it. Where is your gun?' Sam added.

'You are not getting out of this house alive,' yelled Peter.

As Peter grabbed Sam and me, Ben bit Peter. He screamed in pain. Suddenly the police leapt through the door and took him away, and that was the last we saw of him.

Lauren Cooper (10)
Bronington Primary School, Whitchurch

How The Leopard Got Its Spots

Long, long ago when the Earth was young there was a beautiful golden leopard. He was always cruel, hungry, rude and he was a liar. He loved to eat fruit and lie to get other animals' fruit.

One day the wise old elephant called a meeting and said, 'You must not eat the fruit on the mushroom tree.' But guess what? The leopard did not listen.

So one calm night when the moon was full the leopard climbed to the top of the mushroom tree and picked the top most fruit so that no one would notice. He then jumped down and all the fruit fell on top of him. He started to cry and the elephant came and told him, 'You are covered in everlasting bruises.'

From that day on the leopard stopped lying and only ate meat.

The moral is: don't take things for granted.

William Bevan (10)
Bronington Primary School, Whitchurch

How The Leopard Got His Spots

Long, long ago there was a monkey and a leopard in a jungle far away. The leopard tricked the monkey all the time. He made him sad and he would cry.

One day the monkeys decided to play a trick on the leopard. When the leopard was asleep the monkeys came down and painted spots on the leopard.

When the leopard woke up he said, 'What are you looking at?' then the monkeys took the leopard to the pond.

The monkeys said, 'Look in the water.'

He saw his reflection in the water and jumped in and died. The monkeys lived happily ever after!

Myles Davies (11)
Bronington Primary School, Whitchurch

How The Leopard Got Rid Of His Spots

Long, long ago there was a leopard. He played tricks on everyone. He had no friends because nobody liked him. There was one person who he couldn't trick, wise owl. He tried to play tricks on him but they never worked.

One day the leopard was drinking out of the pond when he noticed his spots. He thought if the spots went he would be prettier. So he went to wise owl's house. When he got there the cheeky monkey was there. He said to the wise owl and the cheeky monkey, 'Will you help get rid of my spots?'

'No,' said the wise owl, 'we will not help you.'

'Why not?' shouted the leopard.

'You are too mean! You play tricks on everyone,' replied the cheeky monkey.

The leopard walked out and went to the pond and looked at himself again. He ran back to owl's house and said to them both he wouldn't play tricks on anyone again.

The wise owl said to the leopard, 'How can we believe you? You are always lying.'

The leopard said, 'I promise I won't play tricks on anyone again.'

The wise owl believed him.

The monkey thought of an idea. It was to paint over the spots. So they did but when he had a wash the paint wiped off. The wise owl thought of an idea. If the leopard was kind the spots might go because the spots came when he was horrible. So the leopard was kind. He was king to the gang of monkeys and the lions. When he looked in the river the spots were gone.

Abigail Swain (11)
Bronington Primary School, Whitchurch

The Red-Headed League

That night Sherlock Holmes and I met outside the pawnbrokers.

'Come on Watson, let's get inside and get down to the cellar before those crafty two do,' said Holmes quickly.

We went charging down to the cellar. We found a big tunnel.

'So this is how they are getting into the bank,' said Holmes quietly. 'Come on Watson, hide behind these bricks. Wait and get ready to fire your gun!' whispered Holmes cocking the trigger of his gun.

Then there was a complete silence. Holmes had got police hidden outside the building and the bank so when the villains came they would go into the cellar and then the police would guard the door.

Just at that second we heard footsteps coming down the cellar stairs. There in our sight were Vincent Spaulding and Duncan Ross. They had pistols with them. Then Holmes jumped out and said quickly 'Caught you red-handed.'

Immediately Ross and Spaulding started firing their pistols. Holmes leapt behind the bricks. Ross and Spaulding were still shooting, we were shooting back. 'Argh, my leg!' I had been shot in the leg. I shot back. I got Spaulding. I threw a brick at him and knocked him out. The police came thundering down and handcuffed the villains. I had to get treatment from a doctor because I had hurt my leg. But I couldn't work out how Holmes knew that Spaulding and Ross were the villains.

Mark Mottershead (10)
Bronington Primary School, Whitchurch

The True Story Of The Grotty Goats Gruff

Once upon a time lived a wicked troll. He lived under the bridge. Along came a goat, 'Let me past.'

Yeah, yeah, everybody thinks that, (because when it happened they ran off to the publishers before I got there!) As you've guessed I am the troll. I am not bad really. I only asked them to tiptoe across the bridge. (I work nights at McDonald's) but they either don't listen, are stupid as I first thought or do it purposely. Well it's annoying anyway.

I was sleeping in my swamp bed (it's supposed to be good for you) when they decided to go from the dusty land to the lush meadow in the most annoying way possible, it's just not fair, I know very well they know about the posh bridge. Well this morning I was sleeping when the smallest goat decided to cross the bridge, by this time I had taken to jumping up and scaring them with my slingshot. He ran off and then the second one came along. He screamed a low monotonous wail then the biggest appeared. He's the only one who's nice and swapped me some goat shoes for my slingshot!

Kerry Chaplin (10)
Bronington Primary School, Whitchurch

The Strange Object

'Wow!' Chloe and Claire exclaimed. They loved surfing. It was their birthday and they had a surfboard each. They had been to the Caribbean for their birthday.

Claire slowly came down to the shore, she was hot and thirsty. She stuck her surfboard in the warm sand and went to finish her cool orange juice. 'It's hot out there,' she told her mum, out of breath.

'Claire!' Chloe yelled. She was sitting on her blue surfboard holding a bottle.

Claire swam over and jumped on her sister's surfboard. 'What's that?' Claire said. Curiously, it was a bottle, it had got a message in it. As she pulled the cork out a message floated out and landed on the surfboard. It was a treasure map!

Half an hour later they found the place where apparently the treasure was. Soon they found a box. As they dug further they then found a shiny key. They opened the black lock and saw a silver sparkly ball. All of a sudden they got sucked into the ball and found themselves wearing grass skirts. They met a boy called Cameron. He was teaching Hawaii dancing, the girls decided to join in and say hello to him. He taught them a dance.

Soon they decided to go back to the beach. It was nearly sunset. As soon as they got to the beach their mum had packed the stuff from the beach. Chloe got her backpack of shells and slipped the crystal ball into the bag and went home for another adventure.

Laura Mellor (10)
Bronington Primary School, Whitchurch

How The Leopard Got Its Spots

Long, long ago when there were no men around to bother the animals, there was a mean, selfish leopard who was very horrible to other animals and loved his golden coat. He especially picked on Cheeky Chimp, Ellie Elephant and Sally Snake. He played tricks on them all the time.

One day they decided they would get revenge on him but they couldn't think of a devious plan.

'That's it!' said Sally. Sally had thought of a brilliant plan. Sally told Cheeky and Ellie that they could put mud on Leopard by Ellie spitting mud out of her trunk while Leopard walked past.

The next day they all went to the swamp, to collect the stickiest mud and put it up Ellie's trunk. They went back and waited for Leopard to walk past. When they heard him Cheeky and Sally hid while Ellie waited. Ellie then jumped out and spat the mud out at Leopard and all of the animals laughed. Leopard started to cry and ran off to the waterhole.

A bit later Cheeky went to the waterhole and saw Leopard. He walked over to him and patted him on the back. Cheeky told him why they'd done it and told the leopard to stop playing tricks on them.

A while later Leopard and Cheeky went to Sally and Ellie and Leopard said sorry to all of them. After that they became best friends.

The moral of the story is: don't be vain.

Charlotte Evans (11)
Bronington Primary School, Whitchurch

The Pied Piper Of Hamelin
(The Story Continues)

Suddenly the rocks swallowed the door and I looked at Hamelin and then it had sealed fully. When I looked round I saw a wonderful land with fruit trees and there were so many magical animals like horses with eagles' wings and honeybees with no sting, so I could play all day long. Never any time passed in this land, it was weird and rather scary. Some days us children would miss our family. We tried not to think of them but it was too hard.

We asked the Pied Piper to take us back but he said, 'You will have to figure it out yourself, only I know how to.'

We tried everything but nothing worked. We thought and thought then I came up with something.

'Maybe he wants his 10,000 Guilders.'

Then another boy said, 'Where are we going to get all that?'

Suddenly we saw an old cave and we went to check inside. We saw lots and lots of money and gold, and an old man.

The old man said, 'This is my gold.'

I said, 'I'll make a deal.' And the others started to fight.

Suddenly there was an earthquake and the old man fell down a deep, dark hole. I took the gold to the Piper and he agreed to let us go. When we were out I went to say hello to the boy on crutches, in the end he became my friend.

Sam Torr (10)
Bronington Primary School, Whitchurch

Why The Sun Travels Across The Sky

Once upon a time in days forgotten, it was afternoon and the sky was light on one side of the Earth and dim on the other. There was a sun and a mean moon that loved to play tricks. Moon was shouting names at Sun.

Moon got annoyed because Sun wasn't doing anything about it. Moon wanted to play a selfish trick on Sun. He thought and thought, 'That's it!' Moon exclaimed.

Sun was going dim as night was coming. Moon was getting bright. Moon stood in the sky chuckling.

It was morning and people were starting to wake up. Sun was ready to come up just like Moon had been, but Moon wouldn't move, he stood in the sky shining down on the dark city. People were beginning to go outside and look at their watches to see if they were supposed to be working.

Moon didn't budge. Moon chuckled and smiled an evil smile. 'Are you OK Sun?' Moon asked.

'No!' Sun roared. 'It's my turn to come up!' Sun was angry!

Sun came up and people down below gave a cheer. Moon still didn't go down. Sun began to chase Moon around the sky, up and down, round and round. Sun stopped and started every now and again.

Moon has never given up and that's why Sun travels around the sky, chasing Moon because he stopped Day from living and that's why Moon may be in the sky in the daylight!

Natasha Forrester (11)
Bronington Primary School, Whitchurch

The Big Mean Mouse And The Gay Elephant

Once upon a time when mice were half the size of elephants, there was a mouse called Meany and an elephant called Joy.

It was a sunny afternoon, the birds were singing and the mice were playing with the elephants, apart from Meany who didn't want to play. Meany had one sharp tooth and always used to bite elephants, apart from his best friend Joyful Joy. Joy didn't like Meany when he bit elephants, so Joy brought up an idea so good that the chief of elephants wouldn't have thought of it.

So later that day Joy put the biggest piece of cheese he could find in Meany's den.

The next day Meany found the huge piece of cheese and nibbled and nibbled. Suddenly he couldn't eat much more, not that he was full, but because his tooth was too blunt.

Meany ran as quickly as possible to Joy and told him the problem. 'Look, look my tooth is blunt so if I bite you it won't hurt, see,' the Mouse said.

So Meany bit Joy but his tooth still hurt and the elephant squealed and stepped on Meany by accident. Meany then was the size of a pea, and that's how mice are so tiny with square teeth.

Moral: think before you leap.

Michael Young (11)
Bronington Primary School, Whitchurch

How The Elephant Got His Tusks Back

Once upon a time there lived a big, brave elephant and a small, helpful mouse. The forest wasn't safe anymore with all the poachers capturing elephants for their tusks made of ivory and tigers for their beautiful coats.

One day in the forest the little brown mouse was picking his favourite berries when he heard a deafening bang and a huge thud. *It sounded quite close,* the mouse thought to himself and went to find out what was wrong.

Minutes later the mouse saw a tusk-less elephant collapsed on the floor tangled in a net. 'Has a poacher done this to you?' the mouse asked.

'What do you care? You're just a helpless little mouse,' grunted the elephant.

'Well, if you don't want me to get you out of this net . . . '

'Oh, I'm sorry I do want to get out of here,' the elephant interrupted.

The mouse nibbled and nibbled until he had made a big enough hole for the elephant to escape.

When they got back to the forest the elephant had changed and was really helpful. He became more and more helpful and as he did so, his tusks started to grow back.

The moral is it doesn't matter if you're big or small.

Shannen Marshall (11)
Bronington Primary School, Whitchurch

The True Story Of The Troll And The Grotty Billy Goat

Once upon a time there lived a family and kind troll (oh yeah that's me) and a grotty Billy goat. I'm a poor old troll. Everytime I want to go to sleep that grotty old goat goes tip, tap, tip, tap across the bridge. Whenever I try to stop him people think I'm being mean to the Billy goat but the Billy goat is being mean to me. Come and watch at 3.30pm and you will know how mean that grotty Billy goat is. He has done horrible things to me, there are so many I can't think what they are.

I was about to nod off to sleep when I heard a tip, tap, tip, tap, going across the bridge and it was the grotty Billy goat. 'Will you just stop that!' I shouted in a trembly voice. That Billy goat had to be stopped! So I tried everything but nothing worked.

One day a farmer came along. I ran up to the farmer and said, 'Oh please can you take the old Billy goat?'

'Oh OK, fine, I'll take the old Billy goat.' So off went the farmer with the Billy goat.

I had so much sleep that I felt very happy, but the next day the farmer turned up with that old Billy goat and said, 'I don't want this Billy goat anymore.'

'Why?' I said.

'Because he keeps eating the vegetables in my garden.' So off the farmer went.

I went up to the Billy goat and said, 'Can we be friends?'

'Yes OK but as long as you don't eat me.'

'Yes I won't eat you but don't go over the bridge between 3.30pm and 6.30pm!'

So from that moment we became friends, or as I call it 'best buddies'.

Chloe Price (10)
Bronington Primary School, Whitchurch

How The Leopard Got Its Spots

Once upon a time there was a leopard with the most beautiful golden fur anyone had ever seen. She was proud of her fur but she was also very vain. The worst thing of all however, which all the animals hated most, was her pranks. She was the best prankster around. (To the other animals' misfortune.)

One evening, just before the leopard went to sleep, the wise old owl of the jungle came to warn the leopard with these words. 'If you play another prank on the animals you will be sorry,' and with that he flew away into the night before the leopard even had chance to speak.

The next day the leopard decided to play a prank on the owl. As she prepared the prank, she noticed that she had a big black spot. She licked it but another one appeared. She started to lick frantically, but still more and more started to appear. She licked and licked until she couldn't lick anymore, but still more appeared. Suddenly there was the owl.

'I told you so,' he chortled.

'I'm sorry, I promise I'll never do anything horrible again. Please get these spots off me,' she whimpered.

'I don't think so,' said the owl. 'It will remind you of your promise every day until you die.'

Moral: it's not what is on the outside but what is on the inside that counts.

Robert Platt (11)
Bronington Primary School, Whitchurch

The Pied Piper Of Hamelin
(The Story Continues)

Thirty years after the Pied Piper had played the tune the lame boy was still nine years of age and hadn't grown one centimetre. The boy thought of when the Pied Piper took all of his friends away and left him behind because he was too slow. He walked towards the place where the Pied Piper had left him behind, and when he got there he found a key on the floor. He picked it up and tried it on the door nearby, it worked.

The lame boy walked inside. As soon as he got inside the door slammed shut. His friends saw him and said, 'Is that you? You are the one the Pied Piper called 'the lame one'. How come you haven't grown or aged?'

'When the Pied Piper played his tune it made me not age,' said the lame boy.

Just then the Pied Piper saw the lame boy and in amazement said, 'How did you get in?'

'You dropped your key on the floor, you can have it back now!' squeaked the young boy.

And they all lived happily ever after.

Ryan Price (9)
Bronington Primary School, Whitchurch

A Day In The Life Of A Caveman

The Earth trembles with fear. While dinosaurs roam the Earth, especially the terrifying Tyrannosaurus, I like to draw cave pictures on my cave wall. My family and I eat Erythrotherium, a rat-like creature, for breakfast. I also like to draw cave art on the walls of my cave. We use daggers, spears and axes made from flint. I eat archerias for tea and they're amphibians. We make figures from tusks, stone or wood to give each other for birthdays. We hunt massive water creatures called Dunkleosteus, the biggest and most frightening in the world. They're about nine metres long and they have armoured bodies and long fins and massive yellow eyes, able to turn 360 degrees. They have strong plates of bone in their large head, those are the teeth, they use them to crunch up the fish they eat.

We use dinosaurs' skin for our cave doors, clothes, bed quilts and mats. We use fire to scare any other dinosaurs from taking over our cave. It's very difficult because sabre-tooth tigers are not really afraid of fire. We get our spears and put triangular-headed dinosaurs, called Diplocauluses on them, so any meat-eaters normally eat the Diplocauluses instead of coming to eat us (unless they're herbivores).

We like to watch little calops which are forty centimetres long.

I like to hunt and eat dinosaurs. Yum!

Kyle Burkitt (9)
Churchstoke CP School, Churchstoke

Mini Cooper

Help, I'm going to have to do a handbrake turn. Errr! Look out beep! Oh no, I'm going to roll down there into that river. Oh no, I was supposed to be home at 3pm. It's now 4pm. I will be in trouble. I wish I hadn't gone so fast.

Jack Morris (9)
Churchstoke CP School, Churchstoke

Sour Ice Cream

One scorching summer's day in Shrewsbury, I saw an ice cream store. I hadn't had one for ages, I begged my mum and she said, 'Yes.' (I was so excited.)

I went to the ice cream store and asked, 'Can I have a toffee ice cream?' It was pickled onion!

Oliver Franklin (9)
Churchstoke CP School, Churchstoke

The Big Sandwich

What a scrumptious sandwich with crunchy lettuce, creamy cheese, thin pink ham, green salad and beige salad cream. I ate a bit, and, ergh, a slimy slug, a hairy spider and a crunchy snail crawled out - so I threw it in the bin!

Lauren Richards (8)
Churchstoke CP School, Churchstoke

The Deadly Secret

It was a cold, stormy night when I unlocked the deadly secret. My hands trembled, my hair stood on end, my knees knocked together. I put my hands out and unlocked the deadly secret. It jumped at me, so ever since I have been afraid of custard pies on springs!

Sean Livingstone (8)
Churchstoke CP School, Churchstoke

A Day In The Life Of An Alien!

Me and my space planet Yugopataimian friend were walking through some bright orange trees and purple bushes. In one of the trees there was a tree house made of steel, without windows, and a huge locked door. I felt scared. The hair on the back of my neck was sticking up. There were huge cannons sticking through holes in the tree house. Goosebumps rose on my arms and legs. I was really scared. I was with an alien with giant sucker-tentacles and bright blue fur. It had a scorpion tail and no mouth and talked with echo-location. I think his name was Freck, that's what it sounded like when I asked his name. I touched one of his sucker-tentacles for the first time on this planet. It felt freezing. Green gas floated out of the sucker-tentacles. I looked at my watch. I forgot it stopped working when we went past the ozone layer.

I went inside the tree house. There were ten Frecks in there, beeping away madly. I raced away out of the door, into rotten, yellow seaweed. It smelled like eggs. As long as it was soft it didn't matter.

I slept. I dreamt I was on Earth and playing football for Chelsea. I woke up, and yawned, except it came out as an echo-location. I looked at myself. I was covered in blue fur. It was that green gas! It had turned me into a Yugopataimian! It was strange, being Yugopataimian.

Josh Bradbury (9)
Churchstoke CP School, Churchstoke

The Time Machine

I was in a grey lift with levers and buttons. I was scared. I could not move. Suddenly I stopped, the doors opened, ice was everywhere. I saw a mammoth in the distance. I shivered, not just from cold but because I was scared. I was in the Ice Age!

Rosie Hughes (8)
Churchstoke CP School, Churchstoke

Bungee-Jump

From the bridge I looked down. I was strapped into a harness that was attached to a bungee. It was 200ft to the valley floor. I could see the fast flowing water over the huge boulders. As I fell I could see the beautiful valley walls. The jump was exhilarating.

Guy Stelmasiak (11)
Churchstoke CP School, Churchstoke

The Jump

I began to sweat on the top of the bridge. It was very high. My grip on the bars got tighter. My hands were slipping off. Eventually I went hurtling down at speeds unknown. Then it came to the end of the bungee cord and I went flying up again.

Matthew Owen (11)
Churchstoke CP School, Churchstoke

Dream

I wondered what it would be like if I was rich. Then in a flash I was rich with a big mansion and a water park, a garage full of motorbikes and the top sports cars and a football pitch.

I was devastated when I woke up!

James Anthony (11)
Churchstoke CP School, Churchstoke

A Day In The Life Of My Dog!

I'm Bernie, I live in a house with my family, Gareth, Steffan, Mum and Dad (and we also have some hens which I enjoy chasing).

I'm woken up this morning by the family walking into my room, it makes me cross and I decide to go outside. I scratch at the door for ages, finally someone pays attention and lets me out. I go to my toilet area outside and then have a sniff and run off. The family shout me but I pretend I'm deaf so I can get away with it. When I'm done outside and ready I come in and have my favourite biscuits. I sleep for a while then go outside and I'm let in for my favourite part of the day, lunchtime! I have a bowl of dry food or sometimes meat and biscuits. I go back out again, spending the afternoon in the garden, which is fun as I chase the cat.

Later I bite the oil man, I think it is really funny, he is swearing running round and jumping, but Dad is cross and shouts at me. Despite this I go for a walk, if it's my lucky day we'll go on the bikes. Dad holds me on the lead and I stop or pull the lead until he falls off the bike and ends up in the hedge, what a laugh! When we get back, I have a nap, another day over.

Gareth Rogers (11)
Churchstoke CP School, Churchstoke

My Football Team's Success

Sweat dripped from my face, I was shaking like a newborn baby. I had to score to win: it was all up to me! The whistle blew, I kicked the ball, it flew towards the goalie. The goalie dived, it went straight in. My team had won the tournament!

Henry Geddes (10)
Churchstoke CP School, Churchstoke

A Day In The Life Of Ivan's Homework

The problem with being Ivan's homework is it's really boring; all I can do is sit around and wait to be done which, might I add, happens once in a blue moon! All I have ever wanted is to be done on time so that I can have a rest on the last night before school.

Why, what's this? No, it can't be! It is, it's light, but I don't understand! It's still only Saturday and this is daylight, not an electric lamp. This could only mean one thing . . .

Ivan is actually doing his homework on time!

Ivan Livingstone (10)
Churchstoke CP School, Churchstoke

Down The Track

The hairs on the back of my neck stood on end as the carriage chugged up the track. My stomach turned as I tried to see what was over the edge . . . *Arghhh!* It then slowed down. I felt so ill. I wish I'd gone on the smaller roller coaster now!

Catherine Sawyer (11)
Churchstoke CP School, Churchstoke

My First Riding Lesson

As I walked up the stable yard I could feel my heart pounding. I was excited, but nervous. I heard my name being called. I looked up and saw my pony, Josh. He was dark brown and loved attention.

Since my first lesson I always ride Josh, he's the best!

Jade Morris (11)
Churchstoke CP School, Churchstoke

Chickens

My legs trembled. My teeth crunched. My heart pounded. My mouth hung open. I screamed. There in front of me was a chicken glaring at me with his terrifying blue eyes. He opened his wings. I shot off in the other direction like a rocket. Why are chickens so scary?

Alison Roberts (11)
Churchstoke CP School, Churchstoke

A Day In The Life Of Mrs Farrington
My Teacher

'Argh!' I screamed as one of the pupils flicked an elastic band at me then I heard a faint 'oops'. It came from right in front of me. I shouted at the pupil and told him to stop fiddling. 'Now, as I was saying before I was so rudely interrupted, the stigma of a plant is what - male or female?' to a girl in the back row.

'Female,' she replied.

'Correct,' I told the class.

The morning dragged on. I was glad to make it to break time, let alone the end of the day. I had a cup of tea and took an Ibroprofen for my terrible, terrible headache. The bell rang and I sighed in a 'not now' sort of mood and dragged myself back to class.

I started to explain to the class what they were doing in maths. I then told Abacus five what page they were doing and then added more explanations to Abacus six and seven, and told Abacus six what page they were doing, then more explanation to Abacus seven, then told them what page they were doing. Phew! I sometimes don't know why I started working as a teacher!

Finally I had another break for lunch. I thought . . . *yes!*

I feel quite fed up by now knowing that I have to go back to class to teach. I feel so tired, I thought, *noooooooo!* when the bell rang but I got on with it.

I finally struggled to the end of the day.

Hooray!

Lucinda Roberts (11)
Churchstoke CP School, Churchstoke

Cow Fear

As I stepped in the field I trembled with fear, scared the cow would charge. My throat went tight and I felt like I should run. I went green and felt like I was going to be sick. But then I touched it and I'm not scared of cows anymore!

Gary Jones (10)
Churchstoke CP School, Churchstoke

The Monster

Silence, then Andy felt a sudden shiver run down his back. He looked behind him only to find a huge brown and hairy eight-legged monster with six eyes and it was looking straight at him! Suddenly it disappeared and a tiny spider crept cautiously out from behind the lamp.

Andy Rowbottom (10)
Churchstoke CP School, Churchstoke

The Life Of A Bear

I was a teddy that sat on a shelf getting dustier and dustier every day; nobody could be bothered to cuddle me anymore.

Then one day in early summer my owner was having a jumble sale. She was called Josephine; it was the day after her fifth birthday and her mother told her to get rid of any toys that she didn't want anymore.

'But Mum I don't have any toys that I don't want anymore,' protested Josephine.

'Course you do! Oh, and don't get rid of any of your new toys,' replied her mother.

There I was just sitting there like a squished lemon, thinking back to the day that she first got me, to the first cuddle, the first time she ever gave me a piece of chocolate cake, right to the day the first dust came.

I know that jumble sales mean doom; you usually get bought by a little baby that chews your ears, right off sometimes. (My uncle, Mr Black, had his left ear chewed off right above his skull earring, hope he choked on it.)

Well on that day I decided to run for it didn't I. I'm not stupid for a bear y'know, (not at all like that stupid elephant with its chubby trunk and its daft giant pink ears that used to sit by me on the shelf of discarded toys). How do you think I got here, upside down in a bin?

You think it's funny? Well at least I'm safe!

Roseanne Gregory (11)
Churchstoke CP School, Churchstoke

Landing

I felt scared, chewing a sweet and holding my breath. My stomach somersaulted, my ears popped. I looked out of the window; the ground was rushing towards me. Suddenly, everything went still. We were back on the ground. The worst bit about flying is definitely the landing!

Sam Farrington (11)
Churchstoke CP School, Churchstoke

A Bat In The Night

I lay in my bed and watched a bat hanging from my curtain rail. My body shivered as it slowly spread its wings and started to awaken from its deep sleep. The jet-black creature began to flutter and flew down to rest its sharp claws on my neck, 'Arghhhh!'

Bryony Marlow-Spalding (10)
Churchstoke CP School, Churchstoke

The Championship

I was feeling fantastic. The title was mine, now twelve months later I was being challenged. Here I was fighting to keep my championship. As my heart pounded, the blood rushed in my ears, I brought the barrel to eye-level and shot. The cartridge was shot. I hit!

Oliver Rose (10)
Ettington CE Primary School, Ettington

In The Mirror

In the mirror I can see an old wrinkly face looking back at me, with a smile and a sigh she makes me think of the years gone by.

I remember when I was seven because I fell out of a tree and cut my knee.

My sweet sixteen when I met my first love.

I remember my marriage when I was twenty-two, the confetti flying all over me.

My first child was born when I was twenty-three, he always liked bouncing on my knee.

When I was forty-one I went sky-high as I learnt to fly in a hot air balloon.

I was fifty, half a century old, when I got my grandchildren.

When I was sixty, I retired from being a caring nurse.

I remember my cruise around the world when I was seventy-three, the family and me.

When I was eighty-one my husband died, but that year I became a great-grandma.

I was flying a kite with my great grandchildren when I was ninety-six.

The telegram from the Queen finally came when I was at the amazing age of one hundred.

I've had a happy life, full of once in a lifetime opportunities.

Inside I feel I'm still having my sweet sixteen, but on the outside I know that I am old.

As this ends my life will follow as I say goodbye to my friends and family.

Megan Stanley (9)
Ettington CE Primary School, Ettington

A Day In The Life Of Tim Henman

This is the men's singles final at Wimbledon. I woke up at 8am, I can't believe it's me playing . . .

I walked onto the court feeling very nervous about if I would win or lose. I was playing somebody else who was a good player. We walked onto the court, I put my bags down. We went onto the court to have a practice round so that we could have a warm-up. I was ready. I served my shot, the other man hit it out. I was very relieved that he hit it out because I was losing the game. I served again and again. I eventually won the game. I was pleased to be the winner of the game. I felt sad for the man I played because he played his best but I was too good for him. I shook hands with him. I was the winner on the day.

I went over to the man who was presenting the winning trophy. He congratulated me on winning the match. I received the cup from him and lifted it up in the air and all the crowd roared. That felt brilliant. I picked up my bags and walked off the court.

I was interviewed on TV. They asked me lots of questions like, 'How do you feel?' and 'How do you feel about winning the game?'

I said, 'It was really great to win a major cup. I'm exhausted!'

Nathan Geekie (9)
Ettington CE Primary School, Ettington

Mini Saga

'Hello is that the coastguard?'

   'Yes, how can we help?'

   'We are stranded on a mudbank.'

   'A team will be with you within the next few minutes.'

   The men, who had been collecting shells, were soon rescued. The coastguards said, 'It was all in a day's work.'

Robert Lilley (11)
Ettington CE Primary School, Ettington

The Discovery

News of a strange reptile spotted on a remote island hits the headlines.

A team of scientists are sent to find the Fire scale, by name, has not been seen for hundreds of years, so this could be a good scientific opportunity . . .

Joseph Lucas (10)
Ettington CE Primary School, Ettington

The Big Night

Jane started dancing when she was ten years old. She enjoyed it very much. Jane went up three stages. When she was eleven her teacher asked Jane if she wanted to take part in a show. She worked to make sure that her routine was perfect. The big night came . . .

Ashleigh Cotton (11)
Ettington CE Primary School, Ettington

A Day In The Life Of Georgina My Chicken

I'm up at 4 o'clock this morning with Lanky's crowing, he's burst my eardrums again! The worst thing is I'm at the top of the pile (I didn't tell you, at night we sleep in a pile), and because Lanky's tall his beak is right in my earhole.

Laura lets us out, Harriet (my daughter) is out first as usual. We've got a different type of bird seed . . . mmmm, it tastes like rooster booster. Man I'm really thirsty, just a minute, have to have a drink.

It's about 12 o'clock in the afternoon. I've just had a pain, time to go and lay an egg I think - ahhhhhhh . . . that's better, laying an egg is just like doing a humungous poo! It hurts a lot because you've got the shell as well!

I'm getting a bit peckish . . . get it? No, really I am, I'll go and have a scrape for half an hour. That's better, I'm not hungry anymore. I'm starving. No, not really, just a joke. I got a bit carried away with scraping.

It's now about half six! That's five hours of solid scraping, it's hard work believe me. I think I'm going to go and have a dust bath. Yeah, go and have a nice roll around in the dust . . . lovely!

Lanky's off crowing again . . . that means three hours until bedtime. I'm quite glad because I'm very tired! Right I'm going up to bed, it's 10 o'clock! I'm going to have a quick drink of water and then go up into our house. *Night.*

Laura Woodfield (10)
Ettington CE Primary School, Ettington

Hamster Escape

It was Christmas Day. Lisa was having a fantastic time until the hamster cage fell on the floor and the cage door flew open.

Honey escaped. Lisa chased him and made a terrible mess. She was going to be grounded.

Lisa suddenly stood up and Honey was in his cage.

Charlotte Holmes (9)
Ettington CE Primary School, Ettington

My Mini Saga

Two sisters were going to a mansion most notorious for cats. They were scared of black felines because of bad luck.

On arrival, they saw a black cat, then suddenly, they saw the ghost of their grandfather Albert.

He had been alive when they'd left for their trip.

Bethan Payne (10)
Ettington CE Primary School, Ettington

Lost

I only wanted Mum to follow. But when I turned around she was gone. I searched the streets of millions of people, in the rain.

Two hours later I gave up hope. Then I saw a familiar face. It was my mum. I will never run away again!

Barnaby Galiffe (8)
Ettington CE Primary School, Ettington

Grandad Far, Far Away

Eight-year-old Gemma lives in England. Grandad lives in America.
They write letters, e-mail and webcam often but have never met.
Surprise! Grandad invited her over. She had to wait a week!
After a long flight she reached Denver. America was brilliant.
Grandad is coming to England soon.

Gemma Griffin (8)
Ettington CE Primary School, Ettington

A Day In The Life Of A Tooth Fairy

Jasmine's mother went into her bedroom and drew the curtains. 'Jasmine, wake up! Have you forgotten it's your first day at school?'

Jasmine jumped out of bed, unfolding her wings. She had been looking forward to this day for months. At last she was old enough to join the Tooth Fairy Squad. Her first assignment would be to collect and bring back a tooth for her teacher. She flew off to school where Miss Jackson was waiting.

'Late on your first day, Jasmine? Your first challenge is to search the field where I have hidden two pink teeth. The rest of the girls are already on the second task.'

Inside the hollow willow tree she soon found the first tooth. 'Where do I look next?' she wondered, gazing around.

Suddenly Jack the magpie flew down and started moaning. 'Do you know how this tooth got into my nest?'

'Thank you Jack. That's just what I'm looking for.'

Miss Jackson was surprised to see Jasmine return so quickly. 'Off you go! There are three children in Egglesbury Village who are expecting a shiny coin under their pillows tomorrow morning.'

Jasmine flew over the gardens looking for signs of children. At Red Hill Cottage a dim light shone in a bedroom window. The triplets were fast asleep as she carefully replaced the teeth under their pillows with shiny one pound coins.

Happily she flew back to her mother holding her first three teeth.

Megan Bradshaw (9)
Ettington CE Primary School, Ettington

Mini Saga

There was a couple called Mr and Mrs Jones who lived on a farm. Mrs Jones heard on the radio that London was being bombed and children were being evacuated. She decided to help and look after four children. They had such a good time, they are still friends now.

Ellie Rathkey (8)
Ettington CE Primary School, Ettington

A Day In The Life Of Adam The Rugby Player

At 7.30 I get up and go into the bathroom and have a shower, then I get dressed. I go downstairs to get breakfast. My wife and my son, Alex, are already down there eating breakfast. It is Friday, Alex's best day of the school week. Then I go and pack my bag to go down to the rugby field. I go outside and walk over to my car and put my bag and balls into my car and drive to the rugby field. When I get there all the other players are arriving too. I get my rugby balls out and start to play.

At 2.30pm I start to sign some autographs. It gets boring sometimes so I only do half an hour but some of the others do an hour. Then I go and do some TV programmes about getting people to play sport to keep fit until 4pm. After that I go home and have time with my wife, have tea and then go to bed.

Alexander Marney (9)
Ettington CE Primary School, Ettington

Mini Saga

Long ago there were five Vikings. They had a plan to take over Lord Sam's town because he was treating all the people badly.

One night they rode into the town and hid behind the bushes outside the castle. By morning they had crept into the castle and taken over.

Hannah Hope (8)
Ettington CE Primary School, Ettington

Friends

Once there was a girl, she loved to play.

She saw someone crying because they were alone.

The girl went to see her. She went to see if she was alright. She was sad, no one wanted to play with her.

'I will play with you,' the girl smiled.

Megan Barnwell (8)
Ettington CE Primary School, Ettington

Day Of Michael Schumacher

I woke up in a posh hotel called The Ritz. I was really nervous, my hand was really shaky because of the championship race. This race meant I would be the six times World Champion. My wife and children wished me good luck.

I got to Silverstone by private jet. It took forty-five minutes. I got in my Formula 1 car. I did the warm-up lap and then I went to the front of the grid. The red lights came on and they turned green. I had a good start but I got overtaken by Jensen Button. I overtook him on the last bend of the first lap. I made my last pit stop and I came out in front of my teammate Rubens Barrichello.

I went over the line, I was on the last lap. I was on the last bend. I thought, *yes, yes, yes.* I went over the finish line. There was a big cheer and my pit lane crew went ecstatic for me. I went to the podium. I got my cup.

Daniel Regan (8)
Ettington CE Primary School, Ettington

The Yellow Light

One night my eyes were closed. I heard noises. I woke up and saw shining lights. I made out the tooth fairy. I remembered I had lost my tooth. The tooth fairy flew over and took my tooth and left a gold coin. In the morning I had more cash.

Sophie Holmes (8)
Ettington CE Primary School, Ettington

A Day In The Life Of Henry VIII

As I woke up I yawned, stretched my legs and got up. My servant dressed me in my gold-rimmed dressing robe, then I headed down the grand staircase towards my spectacular breakfast. After breakfast I went out hunting. I used my finest bow and my most accurate arrows. I killed a fierce wild boar and two adult deer. My accomplice brought them all back.

When I arrived home I was welcomed by some servants who accompanied me to my light lunch.

In the afternoon I wrote some letters for the welfare of the kingdom. That killed two hours but I spent the rest of the afternoon having a nap.

When my most trustworthy servant awoke me, I dressed in my formal but incredible robes and crown then headed down the sumptuous staircase towards my exquisite banquet. As I entered the luxurious dining hall I was greeted by the loveliest smell. The boar I had caught earlier was being roasted over an open fire. At my sight the servants tending the fire quickly carved the boar onto the great serving dish. As I sat down with all my courtiers, my favourite jolly music began to play.

After the grand banquet I headed up towards my bedchamber. As I wrapped the silk around me my eyes began to droop.

Jonathan Vestentoft (9)
Ettington CE Primary School, Ettington

A Training Day In The Life Of Jonny Wilkinson

My name is Jonny Wilkinson and I am 24 years old. I play fly half for Newcastle Falcons and have had, so far, 52 caps for England. Since the World Cup I have been injured and am now training hard to get fit again.

Every training day I get up at six o'clock and have a shower and get dressed into my tracksuit. I then have a five-mile run. When I get back I have breakfast which has lots of protein in.

At 9 o'clock I go to Newcastle Falcons' rugby ground where I meet up with the rest of the team. We spend the next two hours doing fitness training. In rugby it is important to be fit.

At lunchtime I go to the club restaurant and have plenty of pasta and chicken to keep me going.

After lunch I go back onto the pitch by myself with a bag of balls and a kicking tee. For the next four hours I practise my kicking. I will not stop until my kicking is exactly where I want it to be.

It is then time to go home and have a shower. Whilst my dinner is cooking I answer all my fanmail, this is a very important job.

To relax before bed I play my guitar. Finally it's time to go to bed, I am exhausted.

This is a typical training day for me.

Daniel Hope (9)
Ettington CE Primary School, Ettington

A Day In The Life Of Shrek

I woke up to the noise of Donkey talking to himself about how beautiful he is, and the sound of Princess Fiona's singing. Suddenly I felt a tickle on my shoulder, it was Donkey's chin hair. I opened the door to find Donkey staring me in the face. Behind me came the princess.

I went down to the river and caught two fish while the princess found bugs and sticks. Then I went to get some leaves. I brushed my teeth and so did the princess while Donkey tried to sing. Then we had our breakfast - fishsticks, bugs and spider cocktails. Then after that we went to a field with lots of sunflowers and as it's on a slope we rolled down it and we ended up kissing. In the background we could hear Donkey coughing, sighing and huffing. We found a caterpillar and ate an end each. I picked a sunflower and gave it to the princess. We skipped slowly up the hill until we reached the top. When we were skipping up the hill Donkey was walking behind us, he was muttering to himself. Princess Fiona was singing what I thought was beautiful, it was high-pitched for an ogre. As for Donkey he thought the singing was terrible and low-pitched, but Princess Fiona thought it was OK.

When we reached the swamp we played hide-and-seek, and me and the princess hid together and ended up kissing again.

Georgina Brooks (9)
Ettington CE Primary School, Ettington

Mini Saga

One day I was in Tesco with my family. We were in the fruit aisle when I saw my friend in the next row. I went to see her but when I came back my family had gone.

I searched for ages until I heard my name over customer announcements . . .

Frances Goss (9)
Ettington CE Primary School, Ettington

Day In The Life Of Jonny Wilkinson

I'm in Sydney today. At 12 o'clock I'm training and at 3 o'clock we're playing Australia in the final. I'm really nervous. What happens if I play like a wally or I'm injured? So we'd better play our best for the Webb Ellis Cup or the World Cup.

Just got off the coach in the practise ground now.

'Right, let's practise conversions Jonny.'

'Right OK boss.'

I put the tee down on the ground and put on the rugby ball. The ball flew straight in the 'H' - I'm doing alright.

Changing rooms: the lads were looking terrified. We had a talk, shook hands with the lads opposite, they looked rough. *Come on Jon,* I thought.

Walking out there was a massive roar. We got in a line. I was in the middle of Jason Robinson and, because I was on the end, I was next to the referee. We sang 'Swing Low Sweet Chariot'.

Eighty minutes past the whistle blew for extra time. I was tired, all of us were, but we had to have another ten minutes. All we could do was to pass it around and attack until Mike Cat passed back to me with twenty seconds left. I drop-kicked, it went high I thought it was going over, it went down. It soared down through the 'H'. I had won us the World Cup.

First they booted it up, as the whistle went there was a mad eruption. England had won the World Cup!

Harry Mace-Hartley (9)
Ettington CE Primary School, Ettington

A Day In The Life Of Peter Pan

Peter Pan is a mysterious person who flies around the sky,
He has no clue how old he is,
And he never tells a lie.

He's charming, kind and magical,
He's easy to understand,
Whenever you're in trouble, he's there to lend a hand.

He saw three children in their beds,
Fast asleep all night,
He crept into the nursery and woke them with a fright.

They flew away to Neverland,
To fight old Captain Hook,
They beat the old big codfish and gave him a nasty look.

'A-ha!' he said,
'You think I'm done,
Well young man it's just begun.'

They drew their swords,
And the fight went on,
'Yippee!' said Pan again. 'I've won!'

He took the children all back home,
'Goodbye,' said Wendy,
Once Peter had gone.

Alice Herring (9)
Ettington CE Primary School, Ettington

A Day In The Life Of A Ghost

Hi, I'm Tom and I'm over four hundred years old. I died when I was nine years old of pneumonia. I still live in my house. Being a ghost isn't too bad because I hear all sorts of secrets and I can even haunt people!

It was late and Ben, who now lives in my house, was wide awake hearing footsteps, a banging door and even his wardrobe would not shut.

As night arrived he went to sleep. Not long after I was woke up by the sound of footsteps. A clock ticked and turning to see the time I realised it was too early for his family to come home from their visit to the theatre. Suddenly the door burst open and there stood a stranger, dressed all in black, with strange, staring red eyes. I froze. I flew towards the window and grabbed the electric wires. Shaking them furiously the house lights kept going on and off.

I heard the stranger stumble down the stairs and stagger across the stone floor in the kitchen and slide under the table. I quickly grabbed some of the family's best china plates and started throwing them at the stranger. Eventually I spotted an old candlestick and chased him out of the house.

That's how I saved Ben's house and family.

Megan Stanley (9)
Ettington CE Primary School, Ettington

Jack's Adventure

Jack was going to France on the Channel Tunnel. At last he was at Folkestone. They got on the train. They were going along well, when suddenly the lights went out. Everyone started screaming and shouting. The captain's voice was heard. He shouted, 'Please everyone, calm down . . .'

Ben Allen (9)
Ettington CE Primary School, Ettington

Help!

One day me and my mates went out on a sailing boat. I accidentally fell overboard but nobody noticed. I screamed but nobody heard me, suddenly something tickled my back. I thought it was a shark - it was a dolphin. It took me to the boat and my friends.

Ben Plant (9)
Ettington CE Primary School, Ettington

Chloe's Adventure

Chloe went to the seaside. She went exploring the rocks and got lost. Her mum and dad got worried. Chloe continued climbing in the direction of what she thought were her mum and dad. She stopped to hear someone shouting, 'Chloe, Chloe.' It was her dad.

Chloe was safe!

Lucy Allen (9)
Ettington CE Primary School, Ettington

Kettle

Here she comes, gets a cup, forgets to put water in me. Brr . . . freezing. That's better, hot water which I like. Argh! She's pouring my hot water out. She's laughing. Oh no, she's spat it out, it's too hot. I sit and wait plugged in and wonder what will happen next.

Sasha Drake (7)
Ettington CE Primary School, Ettington

A Day In The Life Of A Pony

I am a nine-year-old pony and I am a light bay with a blaze down my nose. So that is why I am called Blaze. I belong to Phoebe and she is nine too. I wake up early, when the birds start singing, and I go for a trot round the field, and meet my friends Clumpy, Holly and Legend, who are also ponies. Phoebe arrives at the field and feeds us breakfast of pony nuts and fresh water. She gives us all a pat and then she uses a soft body brush to groom me. My chin moves because I like it.

Phoebe has to go to school. So I spend the day eating grass and chasing the other ponies.

When Phoebe comes back from school I canter to the gate and neigh. She is wearing her jodhpurs and riding boots. She takes me into my stable and grooms me again. She uses a hoof pick to remove mud and stones. She puts on my new bridle and saddle, but I get excited and trot round the stable. We go for a hack up the track.

After this I go back to the stables where Phoebe untacks me, gives me something to eat and leaves me for ten minutes to settle down before she puts my head collar on and lets me into the field. I like this as I can go and play with my friends. Later at night, after I've eaten more grass, I go to sleep standing up.

Phoebe Leathart (9)
Ettington CE Primary School, Ettington

A Day In The Life Of Robert Prosser

One day Robert decided to ride his bike. He was riding up a mountain. He nearly got to the top when suddenly he fell off and rolled all the way down. 'Quick get the ambulance,' he shouted.

His mom wondered what to do with him. 'Where's my mobile, where?'

Ouch!

Dani Szucs
Fairway JI School, Kings Norton

A Day In The Life Of Robert Prosser

Robert went to football practice and won a trophy. He was speeding home on his bike, he fell off and broke his leg. He rang the ambulance and got rushed into hospital. His mom was very worried. He had to stay at home for eight weeks. He missed school.

Shannon Reilly (9)
Fairway JI School, Kings Norton

Mini Saga

Robert went to football practice and won two trophies. He got onto the coach and went home. He told his mum and she said, 'I am so proud of you son. When your dad gets back you can tell him the good news too!'

Hope Douglas
Fairway JI School, Kings Norton

A Day In The Life Of Winnie The Pooh

One day Winnie the Pooh got honey and played with Piglet and friends. They went to the ice park. Winnie the Pooh got stuck in the ice. Piglet was trying to get him out. 'You are too fat.' Piglet went to get some more friends, eventually Winnie got out!

Tori Spittle
Fairway JI School, Kings Norton

A Day In The Life Of Scooby-Doo

Scooby was just waking up when he realised he was in the horridly haunted house on horrifying hill. 'Raggy!' he shouted, but no Shaggy. 'Relma!' But no Velma. 'Anyone?' But no one was there.

Scooby-Doo walked through the door when *bang!* a zombie walked through.

'Here are your friends . . . '

Nikisha Talbot (11)
Fairway Jl School, Kings Norton

A Day In The Life Of Matt From Busted

I opened my eyes, 10am on a school day. I'm not me, who am I? Matt from Busted.

That day I shopped till I dropped. I slept like a baby that night, but when I awoke I wasn't Matt. I was Jessie in my room! What has Matt done?

Jessica Evans
Fairway JI School, Kings Norton

A Day In The Life Of Dopey - Snow White

Dopey walked through the door, never realised something - *surprise!*

It was his birthday! He had no idea he was thirty-four years old. Just a normal day.

The party was great but soon ended. They were clearing up and the witch said, 'Thank you.'

The party was *surprising!*

Charlotte Jenkins (11)
Fairway JI School, Kings Norton

A Day In The Life Of Scooby-Doo

Scooby walked through a graveyard with Shaggy. It got dark and Scooby heard noises by his feet. He was standing on a grave. A zombie popped out of the ground. It chased them but they hid behind a bush. They pounced on the zombie, crushing it to death (once again!)

Danielle Bourne (11)
Fairway JI School, Kings Norton

A Day In The Life Of Danny From McFly

I woke. We were going to our first concert of the tour! I dressed quickly, as I could then make the rest of McFly practice. We got ready for the concert. We got to Wembley.

'Arggh!' shouted Harry. 'My drumsticks!'

I rang a music shop and got Harry new drumsticks delivered just in time!

Jessica Perrin (11)
Fairway JI School, Kings Norton

Tom And Jerry

Tom and Jerry were walking through the field, when Jerry fell down a dip. 'Oh no, what shall I do?'

Tom had an idea. So he got to work . . . but gosh Tom had fallen in. They looked around and saw a ladder. They climbed up into fresh air!

Bhavana Ghai
Fairway Jl School, Kings Norton

Roller Coaster

I had sweat dripping down my body and butterflies in my tummy and suddenly I dropped . . . 'Argh!' I was absolutely terrified I was going to faint. I am so terrified of roller coasters.

Rose Piggott-Smith (8)
Langmoor Primary School, Oadby

The Sea Trip

My stomach lurched; my hair was sticking to my neck. We were going up, down, up and down. The floor rushed up at me and everything went black. I felt really scared and I fell to the side like a rag doll. I wish I wasn't so scared of the sea.

Felicity Roles (9)
Langmoor Primary School, Oadby

Roller Coaster

This was it, I was on it. It gathered speed every second. It did loop-the-loops. My hands were sweating. I came to the finale and at the bottom was a deep, dark hole. I woke up, the roller coaster, it was all a dream.

Daljinder Johal (9)
Langmoor Primary School, Oadby

I Hate Cars

My tummy was rumbling and my head was sweating. I felt like I was going to be sick. It was like I was going to faint. My heart was pounding as the journey went on. I felt like I was jelly on a plate with nothing inside me.

I hate cars.

Emily Bexon (9)
Langmoor Primary School, Oadby

In The Car

I was in the car, my sister was green and she sat up straight. I moved to the other side of the car then my sister was sick and there were green blobs like rocks. It was very, very smelly, then my dad was sick too. *Help me!*

Andrew Harris (9)
Langmoor Primary School, Oadby

Walking My Dog

I was walking my dog with my dad. My dog was running and we were in the dark. I couldn't see my dog. We were looking everywhere. I started to run, I ran fast and I tripped over a stick. I shouted my dog 'Spartacus,' and he came to me.

Danielle Leadbitter (9)
Langmoor Primary School, Oadby

It's A Secret!

There it was again, that knocking noise. What could it be? At first I thought it might be my mum, but she's fast asleep in bed, or was it all in my mind? I was scared stiff. I was so scared that I wet the bed.

Harriet Hewitt (9)
Langmoor Primary School, Oadby

Car Journey

I was terrified, I felt like my head was going to fall off. My hands were shaking. My heart was beating really fast. I had sweat dripping down my body. I felt as if I was going to faint any moment, then finally the car stopped and we were there.

Holly Ilott (9)
Langmoor Primary School, Oadby

Roller Coaster

My hands were sweating like I was being cooked in an oven. My face was as red as a tomato. 'Argh!' I was twisting round and round. I felt like I was going to be sick and I was going to faint any minute. I hate roller coasters.

Ravine Walker (9)
Langmoor Primary School, Oadby

Walking Up The Stairs

My hands were sweating. As I went up the stairs, I took one step at a time, one by one, by one, it echoed in my ear as there was nobody there. Sweat was pouring off me. I was holding onto the black banister and my hands were sticking on . . .

Emma Willson (9)
Langmoor Primary School, Oadby

The Bus

My hands shook, my spine felt like it had snapped in half. I went down the stairs and I held my dad's hand. It felt like my insides were eating each other, then we got off at the stop. That's why I hate going on a double-decker bus.

Reece Ridgway (9)
Langmoor Primary School, Oadby

When I Went To Bed

I went to bed and tried to get to sleep but my bed wasn't comfortable. I kept tossing, turning while I was awake. Suddenly the curtains blew. I went to see what it was then suddenly . . . I felt something on my chest. I hurried back into my bed.

Luke Phillips (9)
Langmoor Primary School, Oadby

Antics

The flashes dart orange on the silvery surface, contained in a large glass dome. He is poised, watching them, waiting for them. He raises a furry limb. Positions it just over the surface. His eyes follow the flashes any moment now . . . *splash!* The cat's paw nearly touches a goldfish.

Kate Nixon (10)
Longden CE Primary School, Shrewsbury

School

It's time to go to school. I walk along the icy path and through the woods. I hear crackling noises and I hear birds squawking. I finally get to school, but when I look at the sign on the door it says *Snowed In,* so I stroll back home.

Louise Smith Ellis (10)
Longden CE Primary School, Shrewsbury

Can I Make It?

I couldn't possibly make it could I? I started to run ten metres, nine metres, eight metres, I was counting down, maybe I could make it. People were climbing on. Four metres, three metres, two metres. I was so close. I jumped, yes, I'd made it onto the school bus.

Laura Wallen (11)
Longden CE Primary School, Shrewsbury

A Day In The Life Of Jonny Wilkinson

It's the big match today, everyone's scared. On the pitch I go to practise for the game. I really hope it goes over in the big game today.

Time for lunch.

'Now men, we've got to get our energy up for the rugby game today,' the coach would say.

I'm worried about the big game today, we're playing Australia, they've beaten us once this year. Then suddenly the horn goes for us to get ready. Then the whistle goes for us to go on the pitch and have a last minute warm up. Then Australia come on. The whistle goes and the game starts.

I kick the ball to start the game off, the ball keeps getting passed to different people. Then I get tripped up and land on my face. The whistle goes. 'Free kick to England,' the ref says. So I get ready to kick the ball, the whistle goes, I kick it. It goes so high nobody can see it. Then suddenly it comes back down so fast it makes a dent in the ground.

Then Australia score, it's one all, then I score ten more. We are in the lead, well until Australia come and take the lead with thirteen but we aren't going to give up.

We get the lead back with the winning goal and everyone cheers for Jonny, that's me!

Lucy Lewis (10)
Longden CE Primary School, Shrewsbury

A Day In The Life Of Funky The Monkey

'Can I have some bananas Mummy?' I said. So off I swung to the best banana tree in the jungle. I was swinging so fast that Mummy lost me. I did not make my trail to get home. So I sat there. 'Mum will come and find me,' I kept on saying to myself.

Finally I stopped saying this and got some bananas. They were lovely. I wanted more but, 'I can't because Mum will be coming soon and I will go home and have tea,' I said to myself. But then down below I saw two men with guns. They looked like poachers, I could not move they would hear. But the wind blew the tree. They looked up and saw me. I tried to get away. I got really far away but they were running fast. I was near my house, I shouted and screamed, 'Mummy it's me, it's me.'

I got home. I saw my mum and said, 'Mum I am really scared. We have to hide, there are poachers.'

We were going to run but we heard their guns. So we stayed until they stopped shooting. We went then but we'd made the wrong decision, because one shot me and the other one shot my mum, then my sister. My dad swung away leaving us to die.

Lucy Hickson (10)
Longden CE Primary School, Shrewsbury

A Day In The Life Of Bozzie

Good morning world, I am hungry, time for a little snack. Yum-yum, but I wish I had grass, oh and dandelions. Ahh, I've started drooling. Time for a little nap. 'Zzzz, buzz, zzzz, buzz, zz.'

Hey what's that? Oh great, a fly, shoo, shoo, shoo, shoo go away. I might as well go for a little nibble of my cardboard house. What's that? Oh no, children now, I'll never be able to sleep, school has started. Hey Miss Jones change my water please? It will only take a minute. She walks past me and gives me a little pat on the head.

It is lunchtime. Oh I am starving. What's for . . . oh same as always, nuts and guinea pig food. Oh what's that? No, no it's, it's . . . it's a lovely person who loves me, coming to take me out. I feel really sleepy. Oh, is it time to go back now? There was a bell sound. Everyone went outside, hold on, but I don't mind, now it's quiet, 'Zzz.' Oh, got an itch. Argh, that's better. That fly keeps coming back, shoo, shoo, will someone come and clean my tank out? I want the flies gone.

At last home time and parents' evening. Oh oh who's that? No, you can't take me, no gotta run, ahhh! Oh no, put me back and down. Hey, where am I going? Hey, this isn't my tank. Next thing I knew I was back.

Maddy Cartwright (11)
Longden CE Primary School, Shrewsbury

A Day In The Life Of Shane Richie

Knock, knock!

'Who is it?' I opened the door.

Flash!

'Uh, what?'

'We're the press Mr Richie, so um, who is going to get married next in EastEnders? Kate, Sonia, Chrissie or Sharon (lovely lady)?'

'What are you asking me for? Ask the producer,' I told them. I closed the door. 'I need to get down to the EastEnders' set,' I told myself. I walked towards the little button labelled 'security'. I pressed. Security came from all doors into the room as a loud voice announced, 'Security.'

Soon my security had got me out of the house. I was speeding into the heart of London. We were almost there. I picked up my shades, and put them on. The Jaguar I was in stopped. I got out. *Flash! Flash!* Screaming reached my ears. 'Not you,' I moaned. It was the press with my fans.

The security pushed their way through the crowd. Finally I was inside the set.

'I need make-up and can you stop those?'

Flash!

'Of course Mr Richie.'

Soon I was on the EastEnders' set, in the Queen Vic. I was acting. Den and Dennis were causing a commotion (as usual). When they had finished I cleaned and washed all the glasses, plates and cutlery.

Kat came over and said, 'Alfie I want a divorce.'

Dun, dun, dun, dun. It was the end of the show.

Jennifer Morgan (10)
Longden CE Primary School, Shrewsbury

A Day In The Life Of A Mouse

Yawn! What's the time? It's quite early, the humans are just going to bed. I think I'll get something to eat . . . I'll have my favourite, cheese! I can smell it now, lovely soft cheese . . . stop daydreaming or that cat will get me.

Better get moving. It's been ages since I set off. Wait there's something coming, oh cat's teeth! Cat at twelve o'clock!

'Miaow!'

That's it, I'm out of here. I think I've lost it, oh no, it's back. I'll try to get it out the cat flap. Here it comes. *Smack!* Ooo, straight out. Hee, hee.

Hey, there's the cheese, oh cat's teeth, it's covered by clingfilm, but I can bite through that. Here I come cheese. Right, now I'm on the cabinet, I can bite through the clingfilm! Yuck, how disgusting. Now I've got to the cheese, time to tuck in!

That was lovely cheese. Right, time to wash it down with the cat's water. Hey, it's almost dawn, before I go to bed I'll root through the scraps of food.

OK! No good! Food there is yucky. I'm going to bed now! Oh no! The cat's here, time to go! Arghhh! It's got my tail. 'Squeak, squeak.' Help! What? It's put me down! Oh cat's teeth, it's coming back. Oh look my mouse hole. I'm in, yes, goodbye cat, hello sleep. Yawn!

Sam Rintoul (10)
Longden CE Primary School, Shrewsbury

A Day In The Life Of Bozzie The GP

Mmmm this is good, my house really tastes nice this time of morning.

'Get out your maths files.'

That's Miss Jones, she's my owner, I'm a class pet so I get all the cuddles. Oh look here comes Emily now, come to free me from my tank and to let me run around on her table. But the time I get the most attention is when I squeal, it tells everyone I want something. That's it 'em up and over, goodbye tank. Please hold on to me. I don't want to fall.

'Emily can you put Bozzie back we have to start maths,' says Miss Jones.

Oh no I was really looking forward to my run around. Ah well I can have a nice sleep now, away from the noisiness of the classroom.

Boom, boom! What was that? Oh it's just Jamie wobbling my house. I think I'll get up and have some food, mmm this gets better and better. These flies are more than annoying, go away. Let's go and see what's in the house to eat. Oh hang on I need a scratch, ooh that feels good, and this tastes good. *Sniff, sniff,* smells like the children are going to have a nice dinner too. Well now I think I'll have another nap until tomorrow.

Georgina Davies (10)
Longden CE Primary School, Shrewsbury

A Day In The Life Of Anubis The Jackal-Headed God

I woke up and went to the jury of judges who judge if people have led a good life or a bad life. There was someone there, he was just going to be judged. Once he had been judged I took him to the feather of truth. I started to weigh his heart, his heart was heavier than the feather. I weighed it again but it was still heavier than the feather, so it meant that he had led a bad life.

Now I have to take him to the main god called Osiris. Osiris makes the decision whether he goes to paradise or the underworld; Osiris has sent him to the underworld. I took his heart that had been weighed and gave it to Ammit who ate it. Ammit is an animal who is quarter hippo, quarter crocodile and half lion.

In comes a different person. I have to do it again, so I do. Her heart was heavier than the feather of truth, but Osiris let her into paradise because she told the truth all the way through the time she was there. I was surprised because normally people will lie because they think the feather of truth will not notice, but it does notice anything bad or anything good - they've done.

I've been waiting a while now but nobody has come. I think I will have a rest 'til the next person comes in so I walk to my bed.

Cerian Abbott (10)
Longden CE Primary School, Shrewsbury

A Day In The Life Of God

I was looking down on the world checking that everything was going according to plan. Everything looked fine down there but up here was chaos! Henry VIII wanted yet another wife. Elvis wanted another song to sing and William Shakespeare wanted to show me his new play called 'Hamlet II'.

Eventually, I had finished watching Shakespeare's play and given Elvis some inspiration for a new song, but for Henry VIII I gave him a dummy wife.

By this time in America, England and Australia people were robbing banks and houses. I had to sort the robbers out by making them into good people. But by the time I have done one person there is always another person.

'I am not amused about all the robbers in this world, there should be none,' said Queen Victoria.

'I'm trying my best,' I said.

'I'm going to do something exciting for once. I think I will move Ireland further away from England.'

'Yeah make something exciting for once,' said Elvis.

'I will, so that it will take six hours to get across in a boat.'

'God, the pray machine is bleeping, you have 1772 prayers to read and they're still coming,' said Angel Gabriel at work.

'Thank you, can you go and invite the people to come in who have just arrived?' I said.

People are arriving here all the time but at least people are being born all the time. I have another night now to sort out the robbers.

Becky Griffiths (11)
Longden CE Primary School, Shrewsbury

A Day In The Life Of An Assassin

I was waiting for the all-clear, I was about to parachute out of the plane. I was being sent to take out Thuddess Valentine, the mass drug dealer. I was being paid £100,000 for this job, it was worth it. I jumped. Let out my parachute and glided down silently. I landed with a slight thud. I started to creep round the back of the building. I saw a guard, he seemed to be coming straight up to me. I took him out silently with one swipe of my sword. 'That's the guard down, now just to get in and kill Valentine,' I whispered to myself.

I saw a wooden door with iron hinges. I entered. I crept up some stairs and through another door I heard someone shout, 'Hey!' I looked round to see a guard. I quickly took my silenced gun, *phut,* he was dead. I hid his body under the stairs and moved on.

I went into Valentine's private quarters which were guarded by two guards. I was the last thing they ever saw. They were dead. I crept in and I saw him, the famous drug dealer. I took my silenced gun, I was about to pull the trigger when he turned round and saw me, he was holding a gun, we both shot. I got him but he got me too, we were both dead.

Stephen Raymond (11)
Longden CE Primary School, Shrewsbury

A Day In The Life Of Smokey The Cat

Get out of someone's bed, go downstairs, wait for food. Listen. Someone's coming, it's about time too. Mmmm, lovely breakfast, chicken and leftovers from last night's tea.

I want to go outside now and find a present for my owners. (Sometimes I don't think they like my presents.) How will I get out of this room? I hear someone coming, they open the door and let me out. Oh no, it's the heavy-breathing dog, run, run, run. I run down the garden and onto the fence. I think I will just lie in the sun and relax for a while.

Suddenly something wakes me up, a sound a bit like a mouse, a mouse I can just about see. I am ready to pounce when I hear one of my owners.

'Smokey, Smokey.'

Oh no, I've got to go in, I pounce and get it. I bring it to my owner.

'Oh Smokey,' says my owner. I don't think she likes it.

It's time for dinner, yum-yum, my favourite, chicken and gravy. After dinner I have a nap, wake up, go outside to find a new present (maybe a bird this time). I see my present, it is a couple of metres away from me. I got it. I leave it in front of the door, come inside and sleep.

Josie Murtha (10)
Longden CE Primary School, Shrewsbury

A Day In The Life Of A Germ

I was born under a fingernail one day in September, and I made a friend called Salmonella. We talked about ourselves and how we got here. Salmonella came from a turkey left out in the sun on a table.

'I was having the most lovely of feasts,' moaned Salmonella.

'Talking about feasts, I'm starving,' I said.

The fingernail which I was on went into wet, damp, brown stuff, melted chocolate. Then the fingers were being sucked.

'Hold on Salmonella,' I yelled. But when I looked the brown was gone and so was my friend.

All of a sudden a white sheet covered me and so I caught my breath back. The cloth started to rub and I split in half, I doubled, I jumped onto the cloth, well I tried to but I fell onto a chip. 'Yum-yum!' I yelled. *Chomp! Chomp! Chomp!* I started eating furiously.

After I'd filled myself up I walked away from the chip and jumped onto some pork, it was so spongy, so I had a sleep.

After an hour I woke up when the pork was being lifted up. I was going in the boiling pan. I ran as fast as I could and jumped onto the hand. I said 'hello' to all the other germs and made myself comfy. The hand was warm and soft, but I got caught on a door handle and waited.

Another hour passed and a rough hand came down on top of me and nearly squashed me. I hung onto the hand for dear life, I fell off and into a bowl of water and soap. Round, down, *glug! Glug! Glug!* Down the plug.

Emily Cox (11)
Longden CE Primary School, Shrewsbury

A Day In The Life Of Reggie The Rat

I am eating some carrot and mixed fruit. Mmmm that was good I love fruit and vegetables. I think I am going to swing on my swingy tube for a little while. Phew, I'm tired, I think I am going to have a rest now.

Hey there are two hands in my tank. I wonder what they are doing? I hope they get out soon because I don't like it. Hey they are picking me up. I hope they put me down. *Where am I going?* I think.

I have just been put on a soft, comfy thing. What can it be? 'Come here Reggie,' says something. Suddenly the thing picks me up and puts me back into my home.

After all of that I have a long drink, a bit of my carrot and mixed fruit, then fall asleep for the rest of the long, tired day.

Laura Price (9)
Longden CE Primary School, Shrewsbury

The Dark Life Of A Five Pound Note

I lay in the till, helplessly, eternal darkness surrounded me as I slept on the metalllic surface, trapped by a long pole. Suddenly light flooded in and the familiar voice of the shopkeeper could be heard . . . 'Five pounds, seventy-two change.'

The shopkeeper handed me over to the customer. I felt overjoyed. I forever wanted to be out of the blackness, however my hopes were short-lived. Within seconds I was locked in a wallet.

After several minutes we arrived at a cinema. 'Oh no!' I shouted as the customer walked towards a drinks machine. He reached out for me. I felt his sweaty grasp as he folded me into a small rectangle, then he pushed me through a slot. I tried to hang on, but it didn't work . . .

Karanjeet Dhesi (11)
Moorgate Primary School, Tamworth

My Trip As A Five Pound Note

I am a five pound note. I have been used to buy a train ticket to Manchester, and now I am in the till.

'Two tickets to Blackpool please,' said the next customer.

'£5 please,' said the cashier, opening the till holding a £10 note. As I was top on the £5 note pile, I was the change. He handed me to the lady.

When I was in Blackpool the lady and her husband wanted donuts, so they paid the person at the donut stall £5. The second the lady took me out of her purse I could smell sweet, sugary donuts. When the lady handed me to the other person I could see the donuts rolling over a type of grill. I went in a clear box full of coins and other notes. Then a small boy came into the back of the stall and said he was bored. He sat on a chair and asked if he could have some money to go up Blackpool Tower. Then the man took me out of the pot and gave me to the boy.

He went out the back door and walked across the road to the tower. He went into the entrance door and paid the man at the till with me. The same as when I was at the till in the train station happened, I was the change for the next person. They went up the tower and then came back down again. I didn't see any of the tower because I was always in the wallet.

The person then went back to the train station and paid for a return ticket back to Birmingham. I was back where I started, at the train station. Now I would relive my day somewhere else . . .

Ben Pickering (9)
Moorgate Primary School, Tamworth

The Great Escape

This is getting really annoying, being bashed around in this pocket with heavy coins on me, sweets and wrappers, and laces, which are meant to be on your shoe.

Oh, we've stopped! Here we go, being passed over to another place, this stop we are at the train station, thank goodness, those 2p coins were making me rip. I'm fed up of this! Although I did get a kiss from a girl last week, so I can be appreciated sometimes but not anymore.

In the cash till I see my old mate £10 on the other side, trying to escape like I do. I have a rest for a while as it is a hectic life being £5, although I am pushed up and down as the till opened.

Oh no, I'm being moved again . . . this isn't that bad actually, it's clean, fresh, with no coins and my friend £10 from the train station underneath me. It is still boring though.

That's it! I'm going to jump free. Experience something different.

I land on the floor with the rain pouring on me. I force myself under the bush with wool. It reminds me of being squashed by 2p coins. I start to regret what I've done. I am with all ants, slugs and snails; and I have a torn corner with mud on the Queen's face.

It becomes dark, so I lie there for the day to come. I never see anything like now, stars, no roof above me, and massive feet stamping past me.

The next day is bright, brightest I've ever seen. I admire the scene in the bush as someone picks me up - my Queen's face smiles for me as I thought the moment wouldn't come.

I snuggle up in the pocket feeling grateful and happy, as I am picked up from the pocket again, then given to the train station - just like it was before.

Charlotte Williamson (11)
Moorgate Primary School, Tamworth

My Life As A £5 Note

Hi! I'm your average dirty, crinkly £5 note. My life is tiring. I move house frequently. The longest amount of time I've ever stayed in one home is seven days. That was in the till at W H Smiths. It wasn't very homely, and the £10 note kept giving me grief. Luckily, it went - but got replaced with another tenner - typical. Anyway, I'm happy now. I'm in Auntie Megan's birthday card to her niece Zoe. I hope she doesn't spend me all at once!

Clip-clop, clip-clop. Auntie Megan's shoes repeated. She walked over to the red postbox. It wasn't my first time in a postbox. But this time I was going to Africa! I felt happy and sad at the same time. I could get out of this crummy country and move into Africa. It was a long wait in the postbox and a brown envelope kept winking at my yellow one.

'Get lost,' shouted the yellow envelope, 'I'm married.'

After a small snooze I felt an earthquake. I was being tipped into a brown sack. 'Santa Claus,' I heard someone shout. It sounded like a young envelope.

We got put into a red van. When we finally arrived at the sorting office, I heard squeals of joy. We were going to Africa! We travelled on a conveyor belt and went under a bright light. Then I heard a voice. 'Got one,' it said pointing to my yellow envelope. A man snatched my envelope and grabbed me. My yellow envelope was lost in a great big bin. I felt lonely and was at tear-point. I got stuffed into the man's pocket. That added to my wrinkles. I remembered a wrinkle decreasing cream I saw on the TV maybe that would help them. I wriggled to the bottom of the man's pocket where I met a £10, £5, £50 and two £20 notes.

Lauren Sutherland (11)
Moorgate Primary School, Tamworth

A Day In The Life Of Fudge (My Guinea Pig)

I forced my eyes open as the scorching sun came through the wire mesh door of my cage. I climbed over my tube to reach my water bottle. A slight shiver formed in my body as my lips touched the cold metal.

Last night it poured down with rain. My fur was a shaggy mess and my padded feet were numb. I needed to warm up, fast.

As I reached the door the sun warmed me up quicker than a click of your fingers. Instantly I knew that I wanted to go out and play, and just my luck, my owner Mark was coming to let me out. Whoopee! Freedom at last!

I jumped out and ran into the bushes. I decided that I didn't like it there as I had a shower from the raindrops falling off the leaves as I brushed past them. The stones were cold too, so I ran out onto the grass. It slid between my toes as I drifted lazily through it. How I love playing outdoors . . . !

Jade Soady-Jones (10)
Moorgate Primary School, Tamworth

A Day In The Life Of Bugs Bunny

'And here I come!' Bugs Bunny said.

'What a twister!' I said. 'I wonder what it's like to be Bugs Bunny? ...
Cool!'

Bzzzzzz, poof!

'Cool . . . what's up Doc?' In a flash second I was transformed into
Bugs Bunny! 'Where's my . . . oh here's my carrot,' I rummaged
through my pocket, muttering. *'Yipes the lion!'*

I ran and ran really fast then, *zzzzzzz*. I was no longer Bugs Bunny
so the lion skidded to a halt and plodded off.

'Err, what's up Doc?'

I twirled round on the spot, on the top of the trapeze was Bugs
Bunny! I looked down at myself. 'Gasp, I'm a cartoon . . . *cool!*' So if
I'm a cartoon character I could do a triple twirl then do five backflips
and after do a kangaroo powerkick, let's try . . . easy! Now everything's
simple. From falling off cliffs to being run over by the 931 bus. I will still
be alive. Oh, almost forgot, *'Hi Mom!'* I made to leave but Bugs Bunny
jumped in front of me.

'You can't leave till midnight, Cinderella.'

'Yeah, yeah . . . huh, so I have to be a cartoon, for let's see, errr,
seven more hours, come on!'

I found out a terrible thing and nearly fainted! It was like I was
oblivious and to everything there's a catch, *shame!*

'Well as they say, the truth hurts!' Bugs Bunny sighed.

'Arghh shut up. Ever heard that before? Something could happen,
couldn't it, like it's a cartoon?'

'No,' said Bugs.

I was trapped . . .

Jacob Robertson (9)
Moorgate Primary School, Tamworth

The Haunted Fair

As I slowly strolled through the empty fairground, the rides didn't move, just the sound of the wind running up my spine. Suddenly a moonlit shadow cast over me. I shook in fear. I took a breath and slowly turned around, and there standing before me was a black shadow. 'Who are you?' I said in a stuttering voice.

'I am the clown who haunts this fair. Would you like to stay for tea?' he growled.

'What's for tea?' I said in a stuttering voice.

'You are,' said the clown, in a voice sounding like glass being crushed into a thousand pieces.

My legs started to run with his laugh echoing in my ear. He started to approach me until I came to a dead end. He smiled and suddenly grabbed me by my hair . . .

Mackenzie Ingley (11)
Moorgate Primary School, Tamworth

A Day in The Life Of Gismo (My Kitten)

By now I was tearing the back door down, eager to escape somewhere outside under the burning sun, until my owners approached me. I glared back at them with my beady bright blue eyes. Opening the door I got really excited. I went off racing, off to nowhere. Then my name was being wanted, or was it me who was being wanted? So I slowly crept back to my home.

Suddenly, I was lifted up high and was perched on someone's arm. My soft ginger and white fur was being pampered, then I was laid back down but I flopped straight over to my right and then to my left. I just couldn't find comfort.

I was going to sunbathe on my back instead. Too hot, too hot, I couldn't bear the scorching heat for any longer. I ran and ran away until I came to a halt, as I was almost trod on by some children. At this moment my ginger fur turned out to be gold! At last shade, but what's that? It's circular and purple and very big. I crept up towards it, and as I got nearer, I got more afraid. Eventually I was in front of it, well it was in front of me! I reached out to put my pink-padded paw in it. Ehh I'm wet now . . .

'Come here, come here.' My owner Jennifer was calling my name.

Mmmm smells good, I raced in for my tea.

Wally Chapman (10)
Moorgate Primary School, Tamworth

A Day In The Life Of Skin

'Come here Skin!' Elliot shouted, chasing me round and round the glass table. Elliot was fun! He's always played with me.

Just then Emma came in with . . . mmm . . . my favourite! *Chocolate eclairs.* My eyes stared slowly, I could feel slobber dripping! My muddy paws jumped up Emma's white top, knocking the eclairs . . . *splat!* *Yummy!* All of the eclairs to myself!

'Oh Skin!' Emma moaned.

Elliot came running over. 'Go away!'

I jumped up Elliot, knocking him over.

'Arghhh . . . peace and quiet!'

'Bad dog!' screamed Emma. 'Go out.' Emma pointed to the back door.

I put my sad eyes on and put my head down. *'Out!'* she yelled.

Alright, alright! Keep your hair on!

Outside . . . There was something moving . . . argghh! It jumped. It really jumped! *Oh!* How stupid, it was only a bird! Ha ha! I wasn't really scared. Anyway, there was a butterfly on the leaf. 'Woof!' The butterfly flew away. I chased it round and round the garden, like I did the other day. That was fun. Elliot threw a stick but I wanted his ball! *Crash!* That woke me out of a daydream. *Oh no!* That's Emma's best flower pot!

Just then Antony came out with my food! *Oh yum!* My favourite! As it's Sunday I get leftovers from our, well their, Sunday lunch. I managed to push the flower pot behind the wall and run to my food! I felt myself shaking with excitement.

Thank you!

Harriett Keirle (10)
Moorgate Primary School, Tamworth

In The Dark

I was standing in the dark shaking with fear. My knees were trembling and my heart was pounding. I was sweating. I squeezed my fist. I turned around to hear a voice whispering. I couldn't see who it was. Then my best friend let me out of the cupboard.

Michael Hulme (9)
Moorgate Primary School, Tamworth

Sick From Head To Toe

I was sick from head to toe, you could cut the tension with a knife. Then it happened . . . I was so nervous I couldn't watch. It was getting closer, it curled and then we all screamed . . . 'Yeahh!' But then it came back, it was hit again . . . we won against Switzerland.

Stefan Hunt (10)
Moorgate Primary School, Tamworth

My Moment Of Fear

I was standing outside shaking and sweating. I must have smelt like a pig by then. The door opened and a strange voice called me in. My heart was pounding. I was terrified, wondering what was going to happen to me. It was my turn now to see the dentist.

Bradley Dukes (10)
Moorgate Primary School, Tamworth

The Last Penalty

It is into penalties. My heart is pounding and my body is shaking as the penalty spot is gleaming.

Nervously Darius Vassell steps up to take England's penalty. He shoots. *No!* A save.

England's dreams have been shattered, the Villa striker has missed. Sadly England are coming home.

George Sayce (11)
Moorgate Primary School, Tamworth

Daylight Dread

I was rushing, hoping I wouldn't be the only one getting there with people angry at me. I was worried, worried more than anything. I was biting my nails and hoping no one would hate me like the grown-ups, then I was there. I was late for school, again!

Abi Stephens (10)
Moorgate Primary School, Tamworth

Enee Meeny Miny Mo

I was astoundingly nervous, it was the first time I had done this. All I had to do was pick one, left or right? It was a big decision, it would change my life forever. The sweat was pouring down my forehead. I had to pick my very own . . . puppy!

Simon Dainter (10)
Moorgate Primary School, Tamworth

I Missed It!

I was nearly there, would I make it? Would I miss any of it? My stomach was churning really badly, I felt like I was going to be sick. I really, really did wish I'd make it in time.

Oh no! I'd missed England playing on the telly.

Oh no!

Meghan Owen (10)
Moorgate Primary School, Tamworth

Pressure

Couldn't bear to watch, wondering what was going to happen, things running through my mind. I was standing still, my feet digging in, I was holding my head, the nerves running through my body. I went in, I was upset England had lost the penalty shootout. We were out.

Paul Cotton (10)
Moorgate Primary School, Tamworth

All The Way To The Top!

I was shaking with fear, my heart was pounding. I had never been as scared in my whole life before. I had climbed all the way to the top floor. I felt violently sick. I stood in the room looking out. Arghhhhhh! I was standing looking out the castle tower.

Tanya Lewis (10)
Moorgate Primary School, Tamworth

The Winning Shot

It was placed down. Nervous, my heart thumped, almost hitting my ribs. I looked around and felt like I was isolated in Hell. If I do this, I will be loved by my team, *if* I don't, goodbye good self. I hit it, the crowd went wild.

Essam Aljaedy (11)
Moorgate Primary School, Tamworth

The Thing!

Sweat dripped down my face as something began to follow me. I started to run but the blackness of it chased me. It had got me, there was no way of escaping now. Wait. I looked again, it had disappeared. I sighed with relief. It was only my *shadow*.

Laura Wesley (11)
Moorgate Primary School, Tamworth

Head Teacher

My hands trembled, my head was full of crazy ideas. I felt violently sick. I couldn't go in. I stood outside biting my nails frantically. She came out and I went in with her. I came out so relieved, she wanted me to be on the school council.

Sarah Guise (10)
Moorgate Primary School, Tamworth

It's Coming

I was shaking, trembling. I could hear loud sounds screaming, *bang!* I wanted to run but I couldn't, my feet were rooted to the floor. Someone was coming, *bash, smash,* they were getting closer.

'Come in,' roared a deep voice.

I slowly walked in.

'Everyone, this is the new girl.'

Stacey Latchford (11)
Moorgate Primary School, Tamworth

A Day In The Life Of Milly The Dog

9am: There's Mum in the kitchen weighing out my diet food, I'm only a bit overweight! Great, here it comes, yum-yum, I love food! I'm still hungry I'll go and look in the bin. Oooooh a tea bag and a chicken nugget! Mum's shouting at me to get out of the bin!

9.30am: Dad's calling me for walkies oh I can't because here comes Sophie and Emma, my sisters. Stroke meee, woof, woof. Dad's now putting my lead on bye!

10.30am: Time for a run around the garden. Ooooh there's Barney the cat, my best friend, woof, woof, please don't scratch me. Oh there's Jo, my next-door neighbour, wow, and Rob cutting the hedge, time to escape. Jump, run, run out onto the road and down, no up. There's my other best friend Buster. He's a dog. Oh I can't reach him there's something pulling me.
    'Bad dog Milly, bad dog!'
    I'm back in the kitchen now.
    'Bad dog. In your basket!'
    I know, I'll put on my sweetest face, stick out my ears, make my eyes go really big and tilt my head!

12pm: After a sleep it's lunchtime, yum-yum. Walkies, run, run and a lot of strokes! I think I'll go upstairs, I'm not allowed but who cares! I run upstairs, oh there's the nice rug!

5pm: Snore!

5.30: Wow is that the time?
    Dinner!
    Yeah, scoff.
    'Walkies!'

7pm: What a great day, time for bed!

Sophie Dawson (10)
Northleigh CE Primary School, Malvern

A Day In The Life Of My Little Sister

8am I wake up, and being a little sister I don't make my bed. I creep into my older sisters' room making sure they're asleep. Then I jump on them!

Next comes an incredibly messy breakfast, followed by TV, baby channels, annoys everyone. Then the next sister who talks to me I pinch. They try to pinch me back but I dodge. I fall on the floor yelling, and I get a load of attention from Mum.

After all that drama I get hungry so it's time for lunch. If I find there are vegetables on my plate, I kick one of my sisters. She kicks me back, I accidentally knock my plate and there go all those vegetables.

Now I've had lunch it's time to invade my family's bedrooms as it's a Saturday. It's time for my older sister to get messy!

First goes the homework into the bin. A tidy bed - that's better - messy now. This looks like an important school letter, the hamster will love it for bedding!

Teatime now, pizza, *yum!* Pizza's my favourite, though the problem is, it's always gone too quickly. So, I nick everyone's second helping. Isn't it such a cunning plan, I'm so cunning but cute!

Before bed I snuggle on the sofa, not making trouble. It's weird, after all the bad things I've done everybody still thinks I'm cuddly and cute at the end of the day.

Mary Fleming (10)
Northleigh CE Primary School, Malvern

A Day In The Life Of An Egyptian Woman

I woke up with an itching back. I looked down and saw I was lying down on a straw bed. Looked down to see what I was wearing. I was wearing a long golden gown which sparkled with glittery jewels. My neck, wrists and ankles were covered with bangles. The room was a small room and had a portrait of a Pharaoh whose name was Tutankhamen.

Just then the door shuddered and swung forward. The man who had swung the door open was the same man who was in the portrait who was Tutankhamen. I froze. Tutankhamen was so handsome I fell in love with him. The way he stared at me made me go all shy. The way I stared at him made him go all shy as well. He then got his courage and said, 'So you're Princess Elizabeth?'

'Well I guess so,' I answered. I thought I must be a princess because I'm rich and beautiful.

Tutankhamen and I had a walk about in his palace grounds and then we gave each other a single kiss. But I ran back to the room. I woke up and thought about what I'd done.

An hour later I decided to go to the market to buy something to eat. On my way back I met Tutankhamen and apologised for running off like that. Tutankhamen accepted my apology and we played in the beautiful garden.

Jasmine Mayo (10)
Northleigh CE Primary School, Malvern

A Day In The Life Of Toffee The Kitten

I have a feeling it's going to rain today. I'll stay in bed, just in case. You can never be too careful, that's what my mum told me. There's a huge draught and a door opens, and through it comes breakfast. Nothing beats breakfast in bed, as you may know.

I've finished that now. It's time to explore. I rip the settee and I scratch the bathroom door to shreds. That's great fun, I tell you.

The afternoon comes and the rain is really starting to annoy me. Pitter-patter. I decide to sit on top of the armchair and watch TV for a bit. This gets boring after a while. I try to help with the crosswords but it's no use. That just irritates the mind. I think I'll curl up back in bed and have a snooze instead. That's the best thing to do in this situation.

It's the evening now. I get up to use the litter tray, then I sink into a hot bath and my coat is groomed and pampered. I feel relaxed. After this, I bury myself in sheets, and doze off. I sit up immediately. What's going to happen when they see the state of the settee?

Emma Knowles (10)
Northleigh CE Primary School, Malvern

My Cat

When I walk around my house I feel like someone is watching and staring. When I walk on the street, it seems that someone is following me. I'm scared and frightened. In my garden, it's there, and gives me a sunken feeling in my belly. It's my sneaky, fat cat.

Caryn Bristow (11)
Northleigh CE Primary School, Malvern

Life Of A Cat!

I was sleeping like a log . . . until *smash!* A little rodent knocked a plate off the kitchen table. It was a vole, just as I thought. So I grabbed a cork-gun and shot it first time. To be honest I felt sorry for the vole. His last word . . . *'Ouch!'*

Dominic Lane (11)
Northleigh CE Primary School, Malvern

Beast For A Brother

Slowly, I walked through the street. Lights shone down, lighting the way. Every few seconds, a car would screech past. As I walked through the park, I looked around the corner and there it was, staring straight at me. It was horrible, it was terrible. It was my . . . *brother!*

Jared Maxfield (10)
Northleigh CE Primary School, Malvern

Dark

Cautiously, I walked into the street, trembling. I took one light step. I went down falling, falling. My face was flat on the street. I stood up going forward.

I was nearly there at the house. I stepped inside, it was dark. I heard creaking coming down the stairs. Him . . . ?

Eric Carlen (10)
Northleigh CE Primary School, Malvern

A Figure

Suddenly a crash! What was that? I got really scared. There, right in front of me, a figure of a ghost.

'Argh!' I screamed. 'What was that Mum?' I screamed but nobody came.

It came nearer and nearer it was . . . it was . . . it was . . . a bird. 'Oh!' I giggled.

Amelia Arnold (10)
Northleigh CE Primary School, Malvern

Revenge Of The Evil Cabbage

One day Tom's Mum went to buy a cabbage. Tom hated cabbage so when she got back Tom took the cabbage to the fish pond, dropped it in and ran back to his house.

'That's strange, Tom have you seen the cabbage?'

'No Mum,' Tom lied back.

'Oh well, we will have to have fish fingers.'

After a meal of fish fingers and peas Tom went up to his room and fell asleep.

In the morning Tom went on his way to school. On the way out he went to look at the cabbage in the fish pond. Tom blinked and looked again. There was no cabbage. Little did he know it was coming up behind him.

Later on Tom's Mum got a phone call from Tom's headmistress asking why Tom had not come to school. Tom's Mum was confused.

Just then Tom walked in and said, 'I know where your cabbage went . . . '

Rowan Whitehouse (9)
Northleigh CE Primary School, Malvern

A Day In The Life Of My Cat Steve

If I was my lazy cat Steve I would do this. 'Zzzzz be quiet I'm trying to sleep.' I would say. I would dream of cat food land. Tins of Felix surrounding a soft bed. Then I would wake up and waddle upstairs, having a rest after every step. Then at the top I would stuff myself, but what *no food!*

Back downstairs through the cat flap 'Oh no, I'm stuck, I'm too fat. Miaow. Miaow!' Then my owner would come and pull me out.
'You have to go on a diet Steve,' she would say. The dreaded word d-d-diet.

I would go upstairs. A waste of valuable sleeping time if you ask me. I saw the box of biscuits, it said 'Delicious vegetable chunks'. Delicious my cat whiskers, they were disgusting. So I would go downstairs but that would make it worse because I would dream of food bowls full to the brim with chicken, pork and lamb.

Well that is about all my cat does every day!

Amy Straughan (9)
Northleigh CE Primary School, Malvern

Unexpected Guest

In the 32nd century, a huge fleet of alien starships came to Earth. In total, there were 1,000 alien ships. The people on Earth heard a very strange noise. It was the noise of the alien ships. Then the ships descended from the clouds. People everywhere were screaming, 'Help! Help!' The only sound people could hear were other people screaming and shouting. The aliens were everywhere, from the Antarctic to the North Pole.

By now humans were not safe on Earth. The aliens quickly took over and were, at this point, the dominant species on Earth. The alien ships destroyed many cities like New York and Sydney. The only thing to do was to evacuate planet Earth. Luckily for humans, there were lots of starships they could use. They also had a rocket - luckily the aliens had not destroyed it.

It had been three months since the aliens made their existence on Earth. So everyone flew away, starships from all corners of the Earth could be seen. They found another M-class planet just like Earth. They landed, and made themselves at home.

On Earth, the aliens were flourishing. They were breeding at incredible rates. Buildings no longer stood.

On the new Earth humans were making a missile to send to Earth. When it got to Earth it would blow up Earth. So it was fired and blew up Earth. The aliens were destroyed. It had worked.

Jake Stromqvist (8)
Northleigh CE Primary School, Malvern

Six

'Mum, what's the time?' asked Ben.

'Six,' said his mum.

'Dad, how many eggs were there?' asked Beth.

'Six,' replied Dad.

'Mum, Jenny's birthday's soon. How old is she?'

'Six,' answered Mum.

'We're not getting anywhere because Mum and Dad only answer six, don't they?' complained Ben.

'Six,' said Beth.

Alexandra Smith (9)
Northleigh CE Primary School, Malvern

Jack And The Beanstalk - The Chicken Story

All I can remember is I laid an egg. Then a harp played me to sleep. Next thing I knew a boy was taking me away, with the harp with the giant chasing. We went down a colossal beanstalk. I started pecking furiously at the beanstalk. Guess who took credit?

Myles Cunningham (9)
Northleigh CE Primary School, Malvern

In A Different Dimension

'Mum,can I go play with Harry?' called Simon.

'Well OK, but don't do any more of those prank calls,' his mum replied.

'OK! Bye,' said Simon, and with that he was off down the road to Harry's house. 'Hi,' said Simon, 'do you want to go into the wood?'

'Um I'll just go ask my mum.' Soon after that Harry returned with some toilet roll, some food and drink. They set off towards the wood.

When they reached the wood they stepped through the tangled branches and their happy faces turned a dark grey. Slime was all around them in the trees and dripping on their tattered clothes.

'Yuck, what is this place?' coughed Harry, wiping especially slimy slime off his maroon jumper.

'I don't know but I know I don't like the look of this place,' Simon said, scowling.

They started to walk along cautiously, every squelch and squirt of the slime made them jump. They walked for what seemed like hours on end until they came back to where they'd started. They walked around again and again, they were repeating time . . .

Eleanor Morrison (8)
Northleigh CE Primary School, Malvern

The Attack Of The Evil Vest

One day, in the rainforest, a gang of wimpish grown-up explorers were travelling along, with a two-day-old baby named Bobby Poopypants. They had been travelling for about three months, when they met a karate teacher.

'I want to learn karate,' said Bobby, so he did.

They made camp nearby and whilst Bobby was learning karate the wimpish grown-ups went exploring.

They had been travelling for two hours when they came across an evil vest. One of the grown-ups put it on. His deodorant started to smell so bad that he died and then the evil vest came to life.

Now Bobby had been learning karate for nine hours.

Suddenly the wimpish gang of grown-ups came running in like headless chickens. 'There's an evil vest, it's destroying our camp, we have to stay here.'

The karate teacher said, 'Who are you?'

'I'm this little baby's father.'

'You've got a very talented baby.'

Suddenly the evil vest came in! Closer and closer then Bobby said, 'Have no fear Nappy is here and thrust his nappy at the evil vest with something dirty in it and the evil vest died.

They found an aeroplane nearby and went in it. They dropped the evil vest on top of Mr Blair's head and, no more vest!

Max Howie (8)
Northleigh CE Primary School, Malvern

A Day In The Life Of A Chicken

6am: Yawn! Wake up and start squawking to wake up the person who lets us out. Nothing like a good scratch outside in the dewy grass.

7am: Mmm! Delicious! Today we had squashy melon seeds with squishy worms. Now for a nap!

8am: Snore!

9am: Time for an egg! My favourite time of the day!

Nobody's around to tell me off for eating my eggs! To be honest, I can't see why they mind. I can't help it. I love the wonderful squashy yoke, it's gorgeous.

10.30: Mmm, lovely, I can't get that scrummy taste out of my beak.
1pm: Time for another feed. Chicken food this time. Delicious, powdery grain.

2.30pm: Soon I can have a mud bath. Rolling around in a dirty ditch, lovely! Good for my health, you know!

3.30pm: Yes! Here she comes! She's running to let me out. Woo hoo! Now run for the compost heap. Ah! That's the stuff!

4pm: Huh! Not fair! I got pushed out of heaven in just half an hour, just because she needed to go inside for something!

5.45pm: Getting dark now! Better go and get inside the nesting box.

6.30pm: Time for bed now. Right, get the good position. No! Not comfy, ahhh! That's better! Nightie night!

7pm: Can't get to sleep. Keep on hearing scary noises outside. I hate the dark! Don't know how birds like owls can cope with it. Oh well, better try again. Goodnight, again.

8pm: Snore, snore!

Katherine Stokes (10)
Northleigh CE Primary School, Malvern

A Day In The Life Of A Puppy

I've woken up and, oh no, I need a wee, oopsy, never mind! *Thump, thump, thump!*

'What's going on? Has somebody been a naughty girl?'

Who, not me, I haven't done anything, what! Hey, where are you taking me?

'Has somebody been a naughty girl?'

No! It's cold out here, let me in. Woof, woof. Whine, whine, that's not fair. Ahh, that's better, grrr.

Hey that's not right there are two of me and my owner. That's definitely not right, it's not there, that's strange.

What, where am I? Oh I must have dozed off, never mind. What shall I do now? Ah, I know, I will go outside and play in the garden. Let's get a stick, come on, you can't get me. Oww you got me. Hah! I got it back. I'm indestructible. Oh dear, not anymore!

Time for a walk, yippee! Woof. Woof. We're going for a walk. We have just walked out of the house and I am already excited! Yey! We're going on the fields. Come on, let's go.

'Come back!'

Sorry I couldn't help it! I'm just so excited. It's a spaniel, oh he is fast, hey! He's got me! I'm going to get you. Oh bye, see you soon. That was fun. A stick, yippee! Throw it please, I've caught it! Throw it again, again. Oh! Where has it gone? It's time to go. We're home now. *Bye!*

Amy Minski (10)
Northleigh CE Primary School, Malvern

A Day In The Life Of A Cheetah

I'm very energetic at this age. I'm learning how to hunt and kill. When I'm older I will be the fastest land animal on the Earth. I am a cheetah, my name is Keko. I love playing with my brother and sister.

Mum I got a live gazelle. I'd been chasing the gazelle for a while, then somehow I killed it. I killed the gazelle. I couldn't believe it. Mum was so pleased with me.

It was midday, it was too hot to do anything. Mum was acting nervously and strange. She told us to run really fast to the climbing tree. As I was running I looked back at Mum and there was a lioness. Mum was doing a good job of getting the lioness to move. I was frightened. After hours Mum finally came back.

It was middle of the afternoon. Me, my brother and my sister had a nap. When we woke up Mum had disappeared. I was hungry and so were the others. Mum brought back a wildebeest. We stuffed our faces.

Mum brought back another gazelle and my brother killed it. We enjoyed chasing after the gazelle but I thought I would let my brother try and kill a gazelle.

It was almost nightfall. I was about to fall asleep when I heard rustling in the bush next to me. I was in luck. I stalked this baby gazelle and I killed it all by myself and ate it all. After, I went straight to sleep.

Abigail Smith (11)
Northleigh CE Primary School, Malvern

A Day In The Life Of A Barbarian

Rubbing my eyes I climbed to my feet. Packing up the blankets I reached into my pack for some breakfast and found only three hunks of salt meat. Picking up my bow I set off into the forest to hunt.

After a breakfast of fresh deer I set off to begin my quest. I tramped across the vast plain. I collapsed to the earth. Suddenly I heard a rumble. I looked up and saw a horde of mounted goblins ducking into the long grass and grabbing my axe I sat in wait . . .

I leapt. I heard a scream. My axe had thudded heavily into a goblin's unprotected leg. The leader fell from his horse, blood pouring from his wounded leg. *Crunch!* I smashed my hobnailed boot down on his head. Seeing their leader dead they ran. Taking the ornate elven helm from the goblin's head I searched his pack. Inside were some hunks of fresh meat and a beautiful jewel-studded dagger.

After many more miles I reached the first town. After a drink at the tavern, I left to go back home. I realised my quest was impossible. I must return to my tribe in shame. But on the way home . . .

It was there, a manticore! After a long battle I won.

At home I was met with celebration and lived in pride for the rest of my days.

Reuben Pearce (10)
Northleigh CE Primary School, Malvern

A Day In The Life Of A Mummy

Boo, ha, ha, woo, cough, wheeze. Blimey those corridors are dirty, oh hi I'm Rudolf and these are my mates, Cleopatra and King Tut. Anyway why are you here? To hear about a day in the life of me! OK then here we go . . .

Yesterday I was taking a leisurely stroll to see if I could scare anyone on the way, to improve my job reputation, us mummies aren't just here for display. *Mummies do have jobs!* Carrying on, I was out walking when Tut came hurtling towards me, he panted, 'Next . . . door . . . tourists.' So naturally I sprinted next door jumped into an empty sarcophagus and I howled, 'You are, um, going to die!' After I had stopped groaning Cleo crept behind them and shouted, *'Boo!'* How hilarious, well it would have been if I hadn't been locked in the stupid sarcophagus, grrr!

So I was stuck and my friends tried to smash the coffin in-between laughing their heads off. When I finally got out I was crumbling to pieces and had to go straight to the ward!

At six Tut stumbled into the ward and chuckled, 'Mr Boss wants to see ya.'

I trudged slowly up to Mr Boss' office.

'One Sarcophagus ruined and you found at the scene of the crime,' he grumbled in his hoarse voice. 'So your punishment hmm?'

And now I spend my free time gluing what my friends smashed! *Great,* not.

Isobel Mathias (9)
Northleigh CE Primary School, Malvern

A Day In The Life Of My Hamster

Asleep all day, awake all night. When I wake up I sniff around then turn to the right, I try to find my food, it's up there above me. I scramble up the bridge ready to eat. Now to fill up my cheeks as far as it goes. I'll carry it down, back down to my den. Let's have a go on my wheel, it's good exercise for me, round and round I go, enjoying every second of it. It's getting tiring now I have to stop.

Let's see what I can do, ahh I've got just the thing after all that exercise I need a rest. Over there underneath my bridge I could make a bed. Right then I need to get some sleep, zzzzz.

That's better, I feel okay, now I feel hungry I need to find food but it's so dark that I can't see my own food bowl. Well then I'll just have to use my nose and find a way around this. Let's see, up, left turn right, up again and here we are. I can finally eat, fill up my mouth as far as it goes. But oh no the sun's coming up. I need to sleep fast, byee! Zzzzz. And that's where this story ends.

Charlotte Jakeman (10)
Northleigh CE Primary School, Malvern

A Day In The Life Of My Hamster!

Yawn! I'd just woken up from a long sleep in my nice, cosy bed. Last night seemed different, just a little bit more cosy and snug.

I opened my eyes and the strangest thing happened. I looked around. I could see a hamster wheel, a hamster house and a hamster water bottle.

I climbed into a strange tube, poked my head out of the top. I saw a wonderful sight of food, glorious food and a bottle of water too. Why is the water green? I needed a drink but the only water was green! Humans were coming at full speed towards me. I ran under my bed. I saw the human pick up my water and go away again, phew that was close, I hope . . . argh! She's back so I stayed under my bed. She stuck a clean bottle of water on my cage. I ran to the water and sucked up gallons and gallons of water. I went to the food and had a little to eat. This was a day to remember, though I'll probably think it was a dream. *Wait!* If I don't know how I got here then how am I going to get back? Right as I woke up I was a hamster, perhaps I have to go back to sleep, yeah I'll try that, I hope it will work. So I tried sleeping and . . . *zzzzzzzzzzzzz*.

I had the craziest dream I was a hamster.

Frances Purnell (10)
Northleigh CE Primary School, Malvern

A Day In The Life Of An Unwanted Trespasser

I walked up to the huge, black, gloomy gates of the old crooked mansion of Mrucilla, not knowing that I was ready to meet my doom!

I limped cautiously over to the door. I could hear the sound of shrieking and dripping blood. *Plop, plop, plop.* I opened the door and came into a magnificent great hall with a golden table standing proudly in the middle.

I walked up to the window and looked at the crackling thunder and lightning. I could hear the thudding rain on the roof. Then I saw it. The huge black figure draped in a velvet cloak. All I could see of its highly domed head were its red piercing eyes. Its green menacing claws were enough to make the mountains shudder. Next to it three other creatures stood shrieking as if to call a fifth. Then I heard shrieking from up the illusory marble staircase. It was enough to make Hell shiver.

I ran back down to the gates. The wind was howling. I ran faster and faster but was too late. The door had slammed shut, I was locked in!

I heard a woman screaming upstairs. I came to the marble staircase and fell back down to the floor. I turned around and there it was. I watched the fifth creature of darkness leak out of the misty landing. I saw seven mangled bodies on the floor which soon would be eight.

Rowan Standish-Hayes (10)
Northleigh CE Primary School, Malvern

A Day In The Life Of A Fish!

Here I am, day by day, swimming around in this large, round thing! Being a fish really isn't that fun you know. It may seem fun but all you do is just float there opening your mouth every so often to let out a few air bubbles! Also, every time you swim around the large, round thing you forget something.

For example, last week, I was determined not to go near the filter because I would get stuck up it, and absent mindedly I swam around the large, round thing to eat my food (that drops in through my roof every morning) and I forgot not to go near the filter. So now I have a bruised head and a broken fin. I won't be able to swim for weeks and weeks. To be honest I've never been a brilliant swimmer even though I'm a fish. You see when I was two I got caught up in a fishing net and ever since then I have never ever been that great swimmer.

My best friend Quake comes from the ocean, he is an angelfish and he lives in the big, big square thing opposite me and my large round thing.

I have lots and lots of decorations in my big round thing. Like the mouldy ship that's in the corner, the weed that grows in the middle by the side of the filter and the multicoloured pebbles on the bottom of my tank. Wow! I finally remembered it, *hooray!*

Sophie Cornelius (10)
Northleigh CE Primary School, Malvern

In The Roman Times

Hi, I'm a Roman soldier. My legion is number fourteen, we're always called up for battles about three times a day. We had a real tough one against the Iceni (British tribe) a few weeks ago. We lost over fifty men, but they lost over two hundred. Well it all started when we were at practice, a man came out with a message on rolled up paper. On it was some scribbled writing. Obviously it had been written quite fast, that meant the enemy were close.

I got on all my armour and off we went sin, dex, sin, dex. I was scared to death. In came the enemy - *slash, slash, slash.* A few of the men (on our side) had been on the ground for a while. In the end we beat the Celts men to twenty of ours.

We headed home and that is when I saw it. It was a normal cave, but there were shadows in it. I stepped inside, there was a torch with special shaped coverings. I looked around and there was not a baddie but a cheeky sort of fellow. But the strange thing was he was a Roman soldier!

Ewan Wilson (7)
Northleigh CE Primary School, Malvern

Quest For The Amber Medallion

There were once three kings and together they made an amber medallion, but they fought over it and their greed eventually took their lives. Years passed by and there, in the seabed, where the kings once lived, was the amber medallion. A curious fish took the medallion and soon after it got washed up on the shore and buried under sand.

Three children, Ben, Sally and Sam, were digging on the beach, the sand gave way. They were in a huge room, the room was underwater. They could actually breathe! The room was long, the doors made from solid gold with amber eyes dotted all over. There was not a window in sight, but the room was bright as the sun. They all ran down the room, quite frightened, and pushed the door. They were in a room filled with glass balls.

'Aaargh!' cried Sam.

'Sorry, it's just these balls, your hands go right through them!'

'Weird!' said Sally and Harry.

All of a sudden, the floor opened up to reveal a silverish rainbow pool, with a platform made from gold, coming through the pool. A whirlpool suddenly appeared and sucked the children in with the platform. Luckily, Harry grabbed the platform and they grasped each other's feet and pulled themselves up. All this time they had been spinning round.

'Owww!' They landed in a dimly lit room. On the floor the medallion was glowing . . .

Catherine Fleming (9)
Northleigh CE Primary School, Malvern

Isabel And Her Adventure

Hi, my name's Issy, well Isabel really but they call me Issy for short.

Anyway, one day I had this kind of vision. Of course I was asleep I think. Anyway I turned into my dog. It was really creepy. I was asleep in the doggy bed. Mum came in, she gave me my breakfast then I went outside to play with my chewy toys. Time flew and it wasn't long until I was eating my tea, then I was in my bed.

In the morning I was me again, but it felt real!

Isabel Ellis (8)
Northleigh CE Primary School, Malvern

The Red Devil

One day there were two boys called George and Will, and when they were coming back from school they found a chamber with a devil in there talking to a man with a black and red cloak.

'Who's he?' said Will.

'I don't know,' said George.

'Hey, they are carrying some treasure,' said Will.

'Let's get out before they see us,' said George.

When they got back home their Mum wasn't there at all. George found a note on the kitchen table it said:

'Dear George and Will,

Your mum is being held a prisoner in our chamber. She's a slave and she is beautiful.

From the Red Devil'.

'Wow, let's go to the chamber,' said Will.

When they got to the chamber there were monsters guarding a door.

'Are those monsters guarding that door?' said Will.

'Yes, they're monsters! Why don't we sneak across that plank over there?' said George.

When they were walking across that plank there was something in front of them.

'What is that thing?' said Will.

'I don't know,' said George.

'It's coming towards us, run!'

'Why did you say that?'

'Because he's coming towards us!'

'But that other monster heard you! Now he is coming to get us,' said George.

'But now we can go and get Mum!'

'Mum! Mum!' whispered George.

'George, Will, what are you doing here?'

'Coming to get you!'

'Then let's go!'

Rhys Jones (9)
Northleigh CE Primary School, Malvern

The Magic Newtown (We've Even Beaten Malvern Wanderers!)

Hi, I'm Cameron. I play football for Newtown in midfield. I sometimes score, take some corners, free kicks and even penalties. I set up goals for my teammates and they help me too. We used to be rubbish but now we're excellent, we win every game.

Cameron Heaton (8)
Northleigh CE Primary School, Malvern

A Day With Avril

Hi, my name's Mysti, I'm twelve years old. I'm here to tell you about when I met Avril Lavigne. I won a competition for the best voice for singing Busted's track 'Air Hostess!' It was great fun. First I got a free ticket to go to her concert, then I went behind the scenes, and I'm just about to tell you what happened.

She was in her dressing room, her clothes were great! She wore flared jeans, a blue dyed top, a wristband and loads of cool accessories. It was really her! She had loads of cool clothes she said I could keep.

We then went skateboarding with her friends, brought sweets and went to watch a DVD. We watched 'Shrek 2'. I loved it. After that she gave me an Avril goodie bag, then we played Top Trumps. She gave me a makeover and I looked like her twin. Afterwards she gave me a huge box of choc chip cookies to last a year. Then we had a disco. She gave me two albums, free. Then she gave me a ride home in her limo!

Alexandra Garwood-Walker (8)
Northleigh CE Primary School, Malvern

The Gotcha Pets

Hi, I'm Pinky the cat, today I'm going to take you back in time, when we made the club 'Gotcha Pets' . . .

One day, not so very long ago, I was walking down the pavement when I met a frog.

'Hi,' said the frog. 'I'm Freddy, and this is Disco the dog.'

'Hi, let's be friends,' I said. 'I'm Pinky the cat. Let's make up a club called The Gotcha Pets.'

'Yes let's. OK!'

'It's getting rather late, let's go to sleep.'

'Yes let's.'

Next morning we got up. Freddy the frog looked at the calendar. 'It's concert day today!'

So we had breakfast and got ready. We got into our blue sports car and off we went. When we got there our concert went on for five hours. When we were finished, we were very proud indeed.

Skye Gamble (8)
Northleigh CE Primary School, Malvern

The Great Day

It was a while ago now when I won the chance to meet my hero, Ronnie O'Sullivan. To win this competition I'd guessed how long it took Ronnie to pot one hundred balls. The answer was six minutes and thirty eight seconds. My guess was six minutes and forty seconds. So that's how I won, now I will tell you all about it.

So when the day came I leapt out of bed, got dressed and dashed downstairs for breakfast. After, me and my dad jumped into the car and off we went, to The Crucible.

When we got there who was standing at the gate? It was Ronnie! He beamed down at me. Then he greeted us by saying, 'Hello, I'm Ronnie and I'm going to be hanging out with you.' I was a little shocked at first, because my hero had just spoken to me, little old me, so you can imagine why I was a little shocked.

Then we went inside The Crucible Theatre and Ronnie asked if I would like to play a game of snooker. I said 'Yes!' So we did and he beat me 129/42. We played eight more games (which I lost) but then it was time to go, so I shook hands with my hero one last time before going, then me and my dad got into the car for the last time in a great day! I looked at my hero once more, then Dad started the engine and off we went.

Kieran Jeffrey (9)
Northleigh CE Primary School, Malvern

My Great Day

It was a Saturday morning in the year 2000. I was watching Spider-Attack. Mum called my name. 'What?' I shouted back. Mum showed me a competition in my favourite comic, called 'Snookykids'. It looked good. If you win you could press 1 to meet O'Sullivan, 2 for Hendry, 3 for Davies and 4 for Doherty.

I won! I was about to press one but my brother made me slip so I pressed two. There was a knock on the door. It was Hendry. That's all I can remember. I woke up.

Jonathan Rushton (8)
Northleigh CE Primary School, Malvern

A Year With Avril

Hi, my name is Roseanne, I'm ten years old. Can I tell you a story?

Well it was a while ago now when I won a competition and I went to see Avril Lavigne. I couldn't believe my eyes. I said to her, 'Is it you really?'

Avril said, 'Yes, who are you?'

'I'm Roseanne.'

'Nice to meet you,' said Avril. 'Come in please.'

She'd dyed her hair blonde and was wearing some baggy trousers with a T-shirt on and some really cool trainers.

Then she just remembered that she had to do a performance. When she was doing it I got to stand in the background and sing along with her, it was great. I think it was on a Wednesday, yeah that was right.

I went to the beach with her, it was the best day for me seeing her. *I loved it!*

Lucy Constable (8)
Northleigh CE Primary School, Malvern

The Lost And Found Hamster

Oh, will you shut up Wimble? That's my little sister, she's so lazy sometimes. Look Wimble, you just need to jump up onto the armchair and then onto the window sill. When our food is up there, she can never be bothered to jump onto the window sill. Oh hello I'm Tickles and this is my very annoying little sister Wimble. We're both cats and just love chasing mice. Shall I tell you about the time when I caught my owner's hamster, and made friends with him? OK, it started when . . .

I was just rolling around in the sun in a little hole (that the owner's dog dug up) when I decided to go across the common to the woods to get a bit of shade. To be honest, I was a bit scared. Well, it's dark and a bit spooky but there sometimes is a bit of light that comes through. Well Wimble told me this bit. Well, Wimble was just curled up, oh let's just forget that bit.

Well, Fudge the hamster was trying to get out of his cage so he could get some fresh air. Eventually he did. He went all around the common and the next thing I'd found a little mouse. I chased him all around the common. Then I stopped and I noticed that it was Fudge the hamster. He said to me, 'I got out of my cage and got lost.'

'Let's take you home.'

And Fudge gave me hugs.

Laura Sockett (8)
Northleigh CE Primary School, Malvern

A Day In The Life Of Homer Simpson

Each day my evil sleep-stopper turns on and Marge rolls me out of bed. I go downstairs and have my breakfast . . . mmm, breakfast. Sorry I'm always really hungry. So anyway, I sit down and meet up with my two kids - Bart and Lisa, oh and Maggie. We have a stack of pancakes and some juice or some cereal. Then I'm off to the nuclear power plant to work for Mr Burns - who my baby, Maggie, shot once.

I arrive at work and meet up with my old buddies Lenny and Carl. I am a safety inspector and I work in sector 7G. Don't tell anyone but when I prevent nuclear melt downs, I just get lucky with 'eeny-meeny-miny-mo'.

At the end of the day, me Lenny and Carl all meet up again and go down to Moe's for a beer.

Moe is pretty unlucky when it comes to prank-callers, but to me whoever that little kid is he has got some talent. Did I tell you that my favourite snacks are doughnuts? Anyway, I love doughnuts and chocolate too. One time, when some Germans took over the nuclear power plant, I was daydreaming about the land of chocolate for ten whole minutes.

I come home to my wonderful family except Bart, he drives me crazy. Normally Bart does something like leaving a skateboard on the stairs and I get so angry I strangle him.

And then, soon it is time for bed again.

Paris Tittley (11)
Northleigh CE Primary School, Malvern

A Day In The Life Of Spider-Man

Beep, beep, beep, snored my alarm clock. I swung out of bed to my feet. Glancing over my room I saw my alarm clock. 8.15 it read. 'No!' I cried. 'I'm late.' Putting on my spider suit and flinging a jacket on, I ran downstairs.

On my way to The Bugle my spider sense went off. I turned the corner and there was a burning building. I heard crying, there was a child stuck inside. I quickly changed into my boots and mask and swung through the window.

'Where are you?' I shouted through the flames. There was no reply. My only chance was to put the fire out. I looked around for taps and water mains. Nothing. I couldn't find a single thing. I looked at the window of the top of the next block of flats, there was a water hose. I had to try.

I jumped to the building, turning on the hose. I ran through the house following the cries and putting the fire out as I went. It was in the bedroom where the kid was, his bunk bed, it had fallen on him and he was trapped!

He was a small, young boy, no taller than a metre stick. I hoisted him out of the rubble and scrambled through the rooms, there wasn't a way out. I climbed up the elevator cord to safety.

Billy Owen (10)
Northleigh CE Primary School, Malvern

A Day In The Life Of The Tooth Fairy

Today is a really busy day because we have to get ready to visit a little girl called Hayley. The reason for this is that one of her very special teeth has fallen out, and that one little tooth is extremely important to me because it will help me build my castle of teeth!

At the moment we are preparing the toothomatic, this is how I get to all the different children's houses. I know that may sound strange but I cannot fly because I am not a tooth fairy, I'm a tooth elf!

We are ready to go now 3 . . . 2 . . . 1! We have lift-off.

Screech! We're finally at Hayley's house and we're ready to extract the tooth from under the pillow. For this we will need the toothopullo, this pulls the tooth out from beneath the pillow without waking the sleeping child. Shhhhhhhh! We must be as quiet as mice as we lift-off into the air and through the window.

That was a tough day and it was hard work fixing the toothomatic. Last time the child's dog damaged it! Now we're all back home at our tooth castle and we can sit down and watch a bit of tooth TV in our special rooms, have a light snack like a whole chicken or stuffed turkey. Then we can wash our tooth collecting uniforms and prepare our snug little beds, made of gums and dental floss. And then we can all have a nice rest.

Hayley Roberts (11)
Northleigh CE Primary School, Malvern

A Day In The Life Of My Dog

I wake up. I am hungry. I'm waiting for my owner to give me some food. Every morning I hear a noise. It sounds like water splashing on the floor.

Then it stops, my owner comes in and gives me my other things, but I am still waiting for my food. I lick my lips. My owner pulls my food out of the cupboard and with a fork she grabs the food and flings it in my bowl. I run over to my bowl and start to eat. I gobble it down in one. Yum!

Then my owner goes outside the house. Another day on my own in the cooking place, well at least my owner leaves the sound box on.

The sound of a cat. I bark out loud. 'Woof! Woof!' The cat runs away. Ha! Ha! I feel like Smudge the Brave. Maybe even Smudge the Magnificent. I think I like the brave better. I feel sleepy. Zzzz!

I wake up to the opening of a door. It is my owner. Yes! More food to come. I gobble it down in one. I go outside and bark. My owner pulls me in.

Later that day my owner takes me for a walk. It is brilliant. I run around, jump up and down. It is the best walk I've had in ages.

Now I am worn out for the day. I am very tired. I decide to go to bed. Zzzz!

Jack Richards (11)
Northleigh CE Primary School, Malvern

A Day In The Life Of Boudicca

Monday

I woke up, I heard the warning bell. It was the time to fight. I went to the bucket of wood and started to paint my face. Everyone started to wake up. The warning bell went off again but this time everyone started to panic. So I made a speech, 'Everyone stop!' I went on, 'The time has come. We have to fight for our land.'

Then everyone shouted 'Ya!'

I started to walk round the village to see if everything was okay. I saw people getting their weapons ready, their faces were really decorated. I saw people on their horses galloping wildly round the fields. Then the warning bell went again but this meant they were close.

Everyone got on their horses and galloped towards them, me at the front leading them. I saw the Romans coming towards us. It was extraordinary but scary because there were three times more of them than us. But the rest of my people were not scared luckily.

My fear started to go I kept on saying to myself, 'I am not scared of anything!' I stood next to the head of the Romans. I shouted, 'Fight!'

Everyone charged at each other. Me and the head of the Romans were fighting each other.

The fighting carried on for hours on end, no one was winning. He called up his back-up ground and all of my gang were tired, so we were giving up and the other people had only just started. I was worried the Romans might take over the land in the end.

All of my people died, one by one. My people died of being stabbed, of being weak and so on, until there was only me left. They took me captive and I felt very alone.

The day of my execution - I drank poison. I died slowly and painfully, and here I am now in my peaceful grave watching the Romans talking over my land.

Grace Bowen (11)
Northleigh CE Primary School, Malvern

A Day In The Life OF A Fantasy Story The War Of The Horkins

Komlin flew, wings flat, gliding with the wind towards the glint of 8,000 spears. He landed perfectly on the branch of an oak watching with his hawk eyes. Komlin was one of the Horkin kindred, half human, half hawk. He fingered his sword hilt, his eyes flashed toward the regiment of mounted Dragonlance spearmen. He could tell they were Dragonlancers as their crest was a lance with a lightning dragon wrapped around it. It was time. He flashed his runefang mumir out of its scabbard, it was the signal. 100,000 Horkin rose from their hiding places and charged full pelt towards the Simlen army.

They had been at war with them for twelve years now on and off, but now it was crunch time, they were going to get revenge for the murder of their Phoenix King, Lomoth.

Komlin whirled mumir above his head and bought it, gracefully down through a Dragonlancer's helmet killing him instantly. His army had suffered terribly but the Sinlen casualties were 100% worse. The Horkin army slowed to a halt as the Sinlens ran away in terror. Komlin and his army returned to their home, Horkinsabam, victorious. When they reached their homes, the lush smell of the wild lumabom plant filled their lungs full of the delicious scent of summer, spring, autumn and winter combined.

When Komlin reached his roost his wife Lilan was waiting for him with bated breath. 'I was s-so wo-orried about you!'

'So you didn't think I could handle it?'

Alex Smith (11)
Northleigh CE Primary School, Malvern

She Ran

The horsemen were after her, she was sure of it, the horn had been blown, she was running away.

Her heart was beating, her mahogany brown hair whipped back across her face, she could hear the piercing high-pitched bark of the hounds, they had caught her scent. She heard the clatter of hooves, it was the landlord, he was sending out his orders she could hear people muttering under their breath, it was the chase . . .

The hounds were only 300yds away now, her head was swimming with thoughts. She would never make it to her destination in time. She could hear the riders lashing their horses' necks, they had spotted her. Now she was worried not to go in to the great wood, she had no choice, she had heard many stories of the people that had ventured into the great wood, but she'd had no choice. She heard the clattering hooves off into the distance, she missed her mum and she talked to herself. The chase was not over yet . . .

Next day 2am

She saw the break of sunlight glinting through the trees, *I must have dozed off*, she thought. She heard men's voices again. They grabbed her by the arms, she didn't kick or scream until they came out of the wood. She screamed, she had a glimpse of the landlord, until she was hurtled onto the back of a strawberry roan horse, she was going home to face the consequences.

Georgia Duddy (11)
Northleigh CE Primary School, Malvern

The Diary Of Blossom The Horse

Dear Diary,

As I woke up in my stable the sun shone in my eyes, I heard my owner Wendy coming with carrots. Today I knew I was going in my favourite field with my best mate Trinny who lives next door in the other stable. Oh and I also remember Wendy telling me that Natalie, my best playmate, was coming to visit me. Nat's Wendy's niece. Nat also likes horses and looks after me. She grooms me, tacks me up, tidies my bedroom (stable) and the best bit, feeds me treats. I heard Wendy coming with my lead rein so I would be let out, I had breakfast in the field with Trinny which meant gossip.

As the gate shut to the field it felt as though we were free. Me and Trinny waited all day for Nat. Wendy said she was going to go to Bromyard Gala first, which is like a show.

As Nat came down the road past my field I went mad, it was like an exciting fit for me. When she got out of the car her friend Caryn was with her. It took me quite a while to get used to her but I did, we played pat Blossom all day and that's my favourite game. I felt calm because Nat was there with her friend.

Goodnight Diary

P.S Let's hope Nat will come again.

Natalie Luce (11)
Northleigh CE Primary School, Malvern

A Day In The Life Of David Beckham

The alarm clock went off at 7.30, I stretched then got out of bed. I put some clothes on and went downstairs. I went into the gym and went on the equipment for half an hour. Then I went into the kitchen to make some breakfast for the missus, the kids and me. Ten minutes later Victoria, Brooklyn and Romeo came down to eat then I went into the gym again for an hour while Victoria took the kids to school and playschool. After that I went shopping so Victoria could make the tea.

At 12.00 Victoria and me went out for lunch.Then at 2pm I went to train at my football club Real Madrid. I was there for three hours training for a very important match this weekend. After that I went to go to pick Brooklyn and Romeo up from school, which was ten minutes walk from the club. Then we went home and watched a bit of television until tea was ready.

After tea I helped Brooklyn with his homework, then we put the kids to bed. For fifteen minutes me and Victoria sat around the table drinking wine and talking till the babysitter arrived so that Victoria and I could go clubbing at the nearby nightclub. We were out until 2am in the morning. We drove the babysitter home. When I got back Victoria and I went upstairs to bed.

Olivia Gudgeon (11)
Northleigh CE Primary School, Malvern

A Day In The Life Of Bart Simpson

Each day I wake up and eat breakfast then I catch the bus to school. My school is Springfield Elementary. My sister Lisa also goes to this school. I don't like my teacher, Mrs Krabapple, because she always gives me detention. Lisa is very annoying because she's top of every class except PE.

I use my skateboard to get home, if I don't have detention I arrive home at about half-past three. If I do have detention it's usually 4 o'clock. When I get home I say hi to my mum (Marge) and Maggie, by the way she's my baby sister. For the remaining time before dinner I either go to the skatepark, or go to Millhouse's to play (Millhouse is my best friend who is virtually blind without glasses) or I get found by Nelson, who is a bully, who forces me into doing something that gets me caught by the police.

When or if I get back from where I've been, Marge is in the kitchen, Maggie is crawling around with a dummy in her mouth and, of course, Lisa is doing homework, but I just sit and watch TV until dinner. Each day at half-past five my favourite show 'The Itchy & Scratchy Show' is on (a gruesome show, where a cat and a mouse try to cut each other up). Then after dinner it's bedtime. Bye!

Tom Mackenzie (11)
Northleigh CE Primary School, Malvern

A Day In The Life Of Udain

As the colossal Udain and his mighty war band ventured deep into the dark, dark forest, a shadowy figure appeared in front of them, warning them about mythical natives and domination. But they continued until they reached a series of large pronged stakes decorated with several heads. As they came into sight three men turning into gibbering wrecks ran screaming. Udain turned and reminded the rest of the group of the prize that lay just ahead of them, money, gold, fine crafted weaponry and the elixir of life! Down the path they continued being careful not to stray too deep off course.

After trudging a few miles they arrived near a clearing. They were about to enter the valley of beasts but were confronted by a legion of forest goblins mounted on giant spiders. The warband darted around in a frenzy of clashing steel and blood-freezing war cries. When the last blade had returned to its wielders scabbard and the last carcass hit the floor the blood-raged group or at least what was left of them continued deeper into the clearing till they reached a passage into an underground cavern. Udain sent his entire band of bodyguards in first. Disturbed screams of pain were shortly followed by several mutilated heads rolling back out. Udain ordered his followers to make a turtle formation. Only a few survived at the end of the supernatural dwelling. Udain noticed a large amount of arcane medallions and jewellery on a sorcerer's table. He took all of these and his life was tragically cut short.

Jack Morris (11)
Northleigh CE Primary School, Malvern

A Day In The Life Of A Dog

I wake up early and start to bark. My mum or dad come down and give me a nice tasty treat and then let me outside, for a good stretch and a bit of a run about. I run, pick up my tennis ball in my mouth, run to the door and start barking at them until they play with me. They throw the ball high or long. I try to catch the ball and take it back to my mum and dad. After I just go in and lie on my bed and try to go back to sleep. Every few minutes I poke my head around the door to see what Mum and Dad are doing.

When my mum and dad go to work I am always alone in the house and I get bored because I am stuck inside until Mum gets home, so I climb the stairs and wait halfway up there for a while. I walk slowly back down the stairs and lie down right next to the back door and fall asleep. I don't have anything to eat and just something to drink.

Eventually Mum gets home and gives me another treat. Then we go for a walk around the field which is next to our house. So we go up there and turn left at a gate and I always try and get into someone's garden, if I can find a way in. We go further up and see the animals and I always get on two legs and jump up at the animals and then I run into the water.

When we get back home I lie around. When my dad gets home at around 8pm I always bark at him and he shouts at me. So I lie down and go to sleep.

Bradley Morton (11)
Northleigh CE Primary School, Malvern

A Day In The Life Of Santa Claus

I woke up to find my beard had been shaved off! Mary Christmas was not in bed, so I looked through her drawer and found my razor and my pair of very lucky socks. Had she gone mad? It took me two weeks to grow that beard!

I went into the kitchen where I saw all my elves running round beardless! I called them over. 'I've lost mine too! Now calm down. Go to the factory and chill.'

In the end, when all the elves were gone, I sat by the fire and ate some toast I made for my breakfast. The clock struck 11am and guess who walked in? Mary Christmas, wearing odd stripy socks, a skirt that was too small for her and a halter top. She went out of the room. I couldn't stand one more minute staring at her.

Time had flown very quickly. One minute it was 11am, the next second it was 2pm. I must have fallen asleep. I went into the kitchen. I made myself a very typical English sandwich! Cheese and pickle, yum! Went for a little nap. Zzzzz.

It was dinner time. I wondered what to have. I know! Pie. I like pie. Yum, yum, yum.

I went to bed. and wondered if Mary Christmas was going to come. Got to get some . . . zzzzz.

Rebekah Johnson (11)
Northleigh CE Primary School, Malvern

A Day In The Life Of Julius Caeser

When I woke up I went straight down to the dock. The guards told me the sea to England was clear and that today was a good idea to invade.

I went to call a meeting with the governors in the royal hall. It took a few hours but we decided to ready fifty ships. I then got some holy chickens from the temple. I fed them seeded cakes and they ate seeds until they fell out of their beaks. This was a good sign. I went to the military barracks and called the captains over. I told them to ready a force of about fifty legions, one hundred cavalry and twenty centurions' legions.

I then had a feast laid out with the best wine, twenty roast pigs, horse meat, bird meat, gladiator battles and much more.

For extra luck Christians were rounded up and executed in the coliseum. Then there were gladiators in the arena.

When it finished I went to the armoury to get ready for the invasion. I then went back to the dock where the army was waiting. We got into the boat and set sail.

Soldiers that weren't sailing the ships were resting. I was on deck looking around the ocean. Men occasionally came up on deck to take shifts at sailing.

It took five days to finally see England. We jumped off the ships and were immediately greeted by hails of arrows. They bounced off our large shields. I ordered the advance.

We just held. The Celt soldiers charged disorderly, but we kept beating them back. They fled.

Ben Davenport (11)
Northleigh CE Primary School, Malvern

A Day In The Life Of Steven Gerrard

I had to wake up at 6.30 this morning at a hotel in Liverpool. Training started at 7.30 and to be honest, I didn't really want to go. But my coach insists that it will help my groin strain that I picked up in the last match for Liverpool. I made my way down to the training ground early so I could get some breakfast from the cafeteria our club provides. The breakfast was gorgeous. I had some fresh fruit, which I shared with Michael Owen, and a lovely warm cup of tea. Our manager, Gerrard Houllier arrived at our ground at 7.35 and as he is the manager, he is allowed to arrive a little bit later. He's always doing it.

Our first exercise was obviously to stretch our muscles so that we won't pull any. We had to run around our big training pitch twice and by the end of that I was so tired I wanted to go back to bed. I wish it was that simple.

The next practice that we had to do was one-on-ones. We were split into pairs with a defender and an attacker. As attackers also need to be able to tackle when the opposition has a corner, we swapped around at times. I am a midfielder and the coach took us away to take part in a different drill. We had to practise long passes to each other from one corner of the pitch to the other. I picked my partner to be Dietmar Hamann because I know him very well. We play alongside each other in the centre of midfield in matches. Even though Dietmar is German and I am English, we still communicate very well.

We finished off our training by having a big match involving everybody except the manager. Our manager is now moving into his late sixties and of course he is not going to compete in a friendly match. Our training session finished at 10.00. The manager let us have the rest of the day to relax. I headed off to the massage spa to get rid of all those tight muscles. I have now been at the club for ten years and I have always had the same masseur. It has been an old superstition of mine. We do have a match tomorrow and another superstition is that I tell the masseur to rub the body parts in a certain order. Feet to the neck. Neck to the hamstring and the hamstring to the back.

After I had finished my massage session, I headed back to my house for a little nap. It was such hard work in the training session and in the match tomorrow I will be working like that for ninety minutes. That is if I am picked to start.

Once I had had my nap I went over to Michael Owen's house with the other lads for a football tournament on Pro Evolution Soccer 3. Of course I won and none of the other players even got close to winning it. Apart from Michael who took the lead with ten minutes to go but I popped up with two goals and I won the tournament.

Before I decided to have my tea I went out to the arcade. I won some games but the game I was worst at, and I hate to say it, was football.

Oliver Garfield (11)
Northleigh CE Primary School, Malvern

A Day In The Life Of Winston Churchill

It is 1940 and I am the Mayor of London and I must now lead England to victory in World War II. I have decided to hire more men for the RAF because if we can destroy Berlin they can't hire more men for the army. I am also recruiting more men for the army so we can destroy the German Navy with submarines. Our army doesn't seem to have changed, but just in case I am hiring more men for the army. I am sending our men out to invade Berlin and then sending out the RAF to bomb it this evening. The navy will take submarines and destroy their boats so we can get cargo over to Britain. We also have the Americans thinking of helping us along with the French.

So far we have stopped the Germans invading Britain. We have heard from the Americans saying that they will help us in the war against Germany. So with the Americans by our side we thought Germany wouldn't stand a chance, but it appears that Germany are being helped by Italy. Then from nowhere the French come in firing their guns at Germany and Italy, so we (as in Britain and America) start making a shield. Then we start firing, so we move into Berlin with guards everywhere, so we start firing. The rest of the army go to see if they can free all the prisoners, and get them safely back to Britain.

1945, Britain have beaten Germany.

Jack Knowles (11)
Northleigh CE Primary School, Malvern

A Day In The Life Of Shrek

'Ugg,' I muttered as I sat up in my stench-ridden tree trunk. Donkey was outside singing in his terrible voice, 'Oh what a beautiful morning' before the forest erupted with shouts of 'stop that noise' and 'is it a banshee?'

I then got dressed, a horrible sight, and for breakfast ate a few unsuspecting bees whilst their so-called companions (I prefer to call them lunch) flew away.

Fiona woke up and she got dressed and had her breakfast. She was looking great, she had on the clothes I rescued her in.

She said, 'Let's go hunting.'

We ran into the forest taking Puss and Donkey - well rather dragging them kicking, screaming and scratching. We saw a band of king's men coming to capture Fiona. Fiona then had a brainwave. When the king's men saw Fiona they ran towards her.

'Wrong move!' I yelled, as I kicked them in the stomach. Puss then sank his teeth into the unfortunate men. Donkey started singing and Fiona delivered the final punch to send them scurrying.

A panel of judges then appeared. The first of the scorers said, 'I give this hunting effort 9.5.'

The other judges said, '8, 8, 5, 9.'

'Wow not bad, 39.5 points!'

When we got home I had a mud bath and then lunch which proved quite tasty, but I still went out to lunch. When we got there a waiter guided us to our table.

For starters I had a lobster which was cooked to perfection. For main I had not one, not two, not three, but four boars. Then the rest of the day passed quickly. I slept but when I woke it was night, so I went partying.

Jonathan Howie (11)
Northleigh CE Primary School, Malvern

A Day In The Life Of Johnny English

Morning

Urgh I suppose I'll have to get up for another day of hard work at MI5 well I better get to it. Oh no where is my suit? . . . Ah, where are the tea cups! Ah-ha there they are. Wait I'm late! OK finally, I am in the car now all I have to do is get there. Erm *car* keys. *Ring ring* - 'Hello.'

'Hi M here, hurry up we have a big case on our hands for you to sort out. It's urgent. Oh and you need to bring your laser watch. Bye.'

Ten minutes later

OK, M has just told me to locate the mastermind called Goldtoe and his henchman Oddmop so this looks like a job for Johnny En - *crash - whoops* never mind. Now I need to find where their secret base is and I have thirty minutes . . .

Forty-five minutes later

In the hospital

Well . . . I think I handled that quite well. Yes they may have given me a few broken bones but luckily back-up, and of course my apprentice Boff, came to the rescue. Now for lunch!

Afternoon

(Eventually escaped from the hospital after stealing an old man's wheelchair in the process.)

Well this has been a long day and I am very glad it has ended.

Ten minutes later

Goodnight.

Michael Ellis (10)
Northleigh CE Primary School, Malvern

A Day As Poppy

7am-8am

Hi it's Poppy the Westie here! It's my birthday today and I'm twenty-eight (well in dog years!) So far I'm having a really good day. Katie (I'm her pet and she's my best friend) bought me a new toy bone. It's so cool. Mum and Dad (Hilary and Lee) bought me some treats that I have never tried before, but they're really yummy. I heard them saying they might take me for a run on the hills this afternoon. They told Katie that Natalie might be able to come as well. Natalie is Katie's friend but I like her.

8am-9am

When they usually have breakfast they sometimes give me little bits of toast, but today they gave me some scrambled egg. That's my favourite. Now Mum and Dad are putting the bowls in the dishwasher.

9.30am-1pm

Dad mowed the lawn, Mum hung her washing out. I sunbathed for a while, whilst Katie played in her play area. Then Katie came and played with me.

1pm-4pm

After lunch we went on the hills with Natalie. The two girls played in the park for a while and then ran down the hill to play with us. I had a race with the girls and I won.

10pm

I'm in bed at the moment. All in all I've had a good day.

Katie Harrison (10)
Northleigh CE Primary School, Malvern

A Day In The Life Of A Hamster

I woke up and everything was dark although I felt wide awake and as bright as a button. As I stretched I felt furry and looking at me I was right, my body was covered in fluffy golden fur. Brushing my fur with pink paws I felt hungry and looking around there was a bowl full of different coloured chunks. I tried nibbling an orange one, but it slipped into my cheeks. As I was thinking how to get it out again, a brilliant plan came into my head, if I put lots of chunks in my cheeks I could carry them anywhere I liked. Stuffing them into my cheeks was harder than I thought because you had to arrange them so you could fit more in.

Once they were full I tried getting through a hole in a big brown box filled with soft white squares of tissue. I only just managed to squeeze through the hole but it took a while. One by one I laid them in a neat pile and only then did I start eating. I decided to take a look around and stepping through the hole again I immediately saw bright yellow walls and a red ladder up to a green platform on which was a blue wheel climbing into it. I found it moved or rocked if I moved or rocked as I was running in it. I went round and round making a noise like a baby's rattle.

A few minutes later a human came in turned on a bright light and lifted me out from my house. I tried to wriggle out of her grip but gave in when she tenderly cuddled me and fed me apple chunks, and of course I couldn't refuse that offer could I?

Gently she put me back into my house and watched me run around and I showed her how I could make my blue wheel move, but found I embarrassed myself when I fell down the red stairs, as I was playing I also found a tube going from upstairs to downstairs. First I would climb up the red stairs then I would whoosh down the tunnel and start again.

Every now and then the human would chuckle to herself or giggle if I did something funny. I was happy and I went to sleep delighted with my day.

Bethaney Allbright (11)
Northleigh CE Primary School, Malvern

The Runaway

Sam ran, her heart was beating as fast as it could, she wouldn't dare to look back, she just kept on running. She could hear the footsteps of people running behind her, their voices shouting out loud: 'Stop thief!'

She was sweating, panicking frantically. Sam was worried, she was crying.

She saw the old warehouse at the end of the road. She came up to the warehouse and ran inside. Sam sat terrified in the corner of the warehouse holding her life in her hands. *Thud, thud, thud.* Everything went silent, the policemen were running into the entrance of the warehouse. Three black shadows stood waiting for any sign of movement in the room. The whole ground floor started vibrating, the policemen split up and started walking around the room.

She couldn't hold her breath any longer, she had to breathe.

'Stop!' shouted one of the men. 'I heard something, she is here. She has moved.'

She was crying, you could hear the drip-drop, drip-drop of the tears on the floor. Panicking, terrified she crept along the floor in the pitch-black room. The ladder. Sam crept up it. She reached the top floor, gasping for breath. Sam suddenly felt a cold hand on her shoulder, she looked back behind her.

'You can't get away now can you little girl?'

Rhiannon Jones (11)
Northleigh CE Primary School, Malvern

Spook Train

The thunder boomed and the lightning flashed. Rain fell down in torrents.

'So, are you scared?' Bill asked Peter, a smirk appeared on his face.

'No!' Peter's face was as brave as a lion but inside he was as frightened as a mouse. Half an hour ago Bill had dared Peter to go in the old deserted fairground. But, getting carried away, Bill also dared him to go into the old spooky train ride.

Feeling like jelly Peter slowly pushed open the rusty metal gate which creaked eerily as it swung open. Peter stumbled through the gates squelching in the mud.

'Be careful,' Tamara shouted. She was Peter's girlfriend.

Cautiously he stepped up onto the wooden platform of the spooky train and peered inside. He gulped. Old plastic spiders, vampires, mummy cases and unimaginable monsters stood frozen. Peter had a feeling that someone was watching him. He spun round. There, in front of him, was a clown. He was sure it wasn't there before. He yelped as red lights flashed on which gave the clown a spooky red glow. Peter stared at the clown. A smile spread across its face revealing decaying yellow teeth. Peter jumped back in terror.

Bill and Tamara waited outside the gates.

'What was that?' Tamara asked, a worried look on her face.

They listened for anything. Muffled screams arose from the fairground. Bill's face turned white. He pushed the gate open and ran to the spooky train. *Flash!* A bolt of lightning struck the ride and sparks flew everywhere.

Back inside the house smoke filled the tracks. Coughing and spluttering Peter staggered to the exit but firm hands dragged him back.

'You'll never leave!' the clown boomed.

Mist and smoke filled his eyes as his vision blurred . . .

'There's no one in there boy, it must have been a cat or something,' the policeman told Bill and Tamara.

'But our friend! Peter went in there!' Tamara sobbed.

'There's no one there little miss, you must be imagining things!' The policeman strode off obviously frustrated by the children's blindness.

Bill sat down, his head in his hands. Suddenly, he sat up and stared in disbelief at what he was seeing. Peter was coming towards them with an older, taller man.

'Hi, guys!' Peter beamed, seeing his friends' faces light up with happiness as he sat down beside them. 'What'cha doin'?' he asked.

'We were just sobbing our hearts out because we thought you were dead!' Bill stood up, his knuckles clenched and face as red as a beetroot. He was livid. 'I'm going to kill you, I nearly did when I sent you in the house but now I definitely will!'

'Nearly,' Peter replied calmly. 'You did!'

Bill stared at him puzzled and confused. 'I'll see you later then?' said Peter as he walked through the wall and disappeared into the early morning.

The older man smiled showing decaying yellow teeth. A red nose appeared just before he vanished too.

Rhian Alford (11)
Northleigh CE Primary School, Malvern

A Swap For Me And Thumper

It was a normal Saturday (or was it?) and I, as usual, went out to see Thumper my rabbit. I gave her a carrot and water and was on my way back when someone called, 'Wait Holly.'

I turned around and said, 'Hello?' No one was there bar Thumper.

'Come here,' he said.

When I went over there I suddenly froze and then Thumper was me and I was Thumper.

'Awesome, I'm a rabbit,' I cheered.

'For a day,' mentioned Thumper, the human.

'What!' I yelled. 'Why did you do this to me?'

'You get less attention than me and get shouted at, so eat my food and drink my drink and have my love,' he replied.

'OK,' I agreed.

So I did, and Thumper gave me loads of attention. It was fun until my brother Ben came. He was mean to Thumper. He picked me up and threw me to Thumper who caught me and put me back whilst Ben (who was laughing his head off) went inside.

'How do you stand being thrown like that every day?' I asked.

'Never mind,' Thumper whispered. 'You can be a human again.'

'Not fair,' I whined. 'I'd love to be a rabbit if it wasn't for Ben.'

So in a flash I was a human again and Thumper was a rabbit. I went inside and then pinched myself, it hurt so it was true. I went to bed happily.

Heidi Loveridge (9)
Northleigh CE Primary School, Malvern

The Invaded Cookie Factory

Harriet woke up, it was five to nine! She put her clothes on, ran down the stairs, had a bite of cereal and sprinted out of the door.

When she got to school the coach was just about to leave for the school trip. So Harriet ran as fast as she could and managed to mingle with the other kids. Everyone was excited because they were going to a cookie factory! When they got there they were greeted by the very rich manager of the company! Harriet wandered away from the group (as she always did).

Suddenly she heard an extremely loud elephant noise, then Harriet remembered the zoo was next door. She heard screaming. The elephants had escaped from the zoo! They were heading for the factory and now they were eating the cookies! Harriet knew she had to do something but by now the elephants were playing catch with the manager. Harriet thought she could get everyone to pull the elephants and they just might be able to get them back into their cage, but by now the elephants were playing piggy-in-the-middle with the manager.

Then Harriet had a brilliant idea; if the elephants liked cookies that much she could make a cookie trail into their cage! It worked, the manager was so happy he gave Harriet a reward. Harriet went home feeling very happy, she was even nice to her sister!

Harriet Duddy (8)
Northleigh CE Primary School, Malvern

Diva Dog

Once there was an ordinary dog, who's owner was called Josh. The dog was called Cheeko. He was a cocker spaniel and he had lovely golden fur and it was perfectly groomed.

One day Josh took Cheeko to the park. Then Cheeko chased rabbits and suddenly when he was down a rabbit hole he fell down, down, down. He landed with a thump in a big room of feathers. Suddenly he heard a l-o-n-g cackle. A bent double figure came into view. Cheeko suddenly jumped up and ran, because he could smell something nasty. But he ran into a dead end. The figure came closer and closer and closer and then there was a loud bang. A squirrel had come to the rescue. The witch (for that was what the figure was) backed away and was gone in the blink of an eye.

The squirrel took Cheeko to the latest fun, a *disco!* Every kind of animal you could think of was there. Cheeko started to make up a dance and then suddenly people lifted him high, he was crowned king of dance. The animals named him Diva Dog. Cheeko liked it there, but he wished he could have his owner there. There was a loud pop and Josh appeared and said, 'What's going on here?' Cheeko answered in a long stream of barks and yelps. 'Okay I understand,' Josh said, half muffled because Cheeko had jumped up and now was licking his face.

Suddenly Josh looked amazed because there and then a huge whitewashed cottage had appeared. So Josh and Cheeko lived in that world and were very happy.

Victoria Dexter (9)
Northleigh CE Primary School, Malvern

I Became An Alien

Hi, I'm Georgia and I'm going to tell you about the day I became an alien. It was an ordinary day and Mum had told me to sort out my wardrobe. I was just about to put everything back in, when a green slimy hand pulled me into my wardrobe. I rubbed my eyes to make sure I wasn't dreaming, but sure enough there was a green slimy alien standing straight ahead of me, talking in a strange tongue, I didn't understand.

Suddenly, like magic, I was somewhere different. I started to walk around but I saw nobody and what was really strange was that there was nothing, not even a tree in sight. Then I saw a cave, *what's in there?* I thought. Suddenly someone shouted, *'Human!'* Then another green slimy alien grabbed my arm. I tried to struggle free but it was useless, they were too strong for me. I just let them take me where they wanted. They took me into another cave and turned me into an alien too, then they let me go. I went into another cave and found an aeroplane thing. I climbed in. It was empty apart from a teapot and a couple of rugs. I was about to climb out when I heard voices. I hid in the back under the rugs. I tried to climb out but they saw me. They asked what I was doing and I told them the whole story. Then they turned me back into an human and sent me home.

Hannah Kenyon (9)
Northleigh CE Primary School, Malvern

A Day In The Life Of Jack Wilson

I awoke, another weird day, a day in which I get to finally tell the extraordinary and bizarre tale of where I am and how I got here.

It's July 18th 2000 and something (I lost track of the year somehow or another) and I've recorded the days in my log book, my only manmade possession. At the moment, I am in my dumpy cabin sharpening my spear ready to venture once again into the jungle.

July 20th

I saw something today, in the dark depths of the jungle, a pair of yellow fangs and a face with a giant hungry expression on it, which said only too clearly that it's hungry for blood, my blood, I fled for my life.

August 1st

I crash-landed here, well . . . I think I did, anyway when I did get here, my memory wiped out. I have no memory of who I am and who my family are, if I did have a family.

Wait! I see something . . . w . . . what? Argh! I'm falling! . . . falling! . . .

Ouch! Hang on, not ouch I've landed on something springy, a-a *spider's web!*

'How nice,' said the spider in a chilling voice. 'You're just in time for dinner.'

'Fine, as long as I'm not the dinner.'

He didn't eat me in the end, I thought it a miracle. Oh! Yes I forgot to explain about how I got here, well, I crash-landed here 2,000 years ago, in my spaceship and now, wa? Wa? Argh.

Sam Burbeck (11)
Northleigh CE Primary School, Malvern

The Girl Who Got Lost In Paris

Hi, my name's Sophie and I'm twelve, can I tell you a story?

When I was in Paris, OK I was on the aeroplane eating my tea and we landed in Paris. I was really excited. I hopped off the aeroplane and found my mum and dad and my older sister. My sister's name is Rebecca. My dad's name is Paul and my mum's name is Alison.

We picked up our suitcases and went to the hotel and unpacked. Then we went to the pub for a snack. After we went for a walk and found a fairground. I told my sister Rebecca that I was going on the bungee-jump but Rebecca hadn't heard me. I paid and got on the ride. My mum, dad and sister walked away. When I got off the ride, I looked around for my mum, dad and sister. I thought I'd found my sister but I hadn't. I looked again. I couldn't find them.

'Aaaaargghh! I'm lost!'

Lucy Ellaway-Bell (8)
Northleigh CE Primary School, Malvern

Jonah The Dragon-Slayer

To the untrained eye, the desert looked as it usually did. Cold, desolate and lifeless. However in the treacherous Plain of the Blooded Sands, nothing was ever as it seemed. For there was life in the desert other than the small bone-eating, blood-drinking mice that made the desert their home. The scent of human was unmistakable. The footprints in the desert were five-toed and the main foot was a slightly curved elliptical shape. These were definite signs that a man had been in this area of the desert.

Jonah had been roaming the desert with his brother for five months now. It was five months ago that he had been outlawed from his home town. It was one day ago that the dragon had killed his brother and, in doing so, taken the life of his last remaining family member. The rest of his family had been carried off by the dragon years ago, but none of them had died of anything other than old age until Jonah was born. He was bad luck to be with. He wanted to die as well, but Fate always seemed to keep him alive, toying with him, teasing him.

However, Jonah had one objective in life. To slay the monster responsible for Jonah becoming an orphan.

Obsidian was a black dragon. He was feared by all. Nobody had ever defied him and, in his opinion, nobody ever would. He was the last of his kind and Jonah was desperate to kill him.

Jonah finally reached the huge, black, scaly mound in the sand at midday. It slowly rose up and down snoring slowly. This was Jonah's last chance and, drawing his lethal dagger and fingering the lucky charms at his neck, he advanced slowly forward.

But as the sun suddenly moved behind a dark cloud, the dragon's eyes flicked open. Its beady purple eyes rolled around - and landed on Jonah. With an almighty roar, the dragon's wings became a blur of movement. A jet of acid green flame shot out from his mouth, just scorching Jonah's hair.

Jonah grabbed his knife - his last weapon - and threw it. It flew straight and true - right into the dragon's soft leathery underbelly. The dragon gave a high-pitched screech and started toppling to the sand. But, in its death throes, it managed to pull Jonah towards it, its claws gouging his stomach. Together they toppled towards the ground.

The full moon shone down on the dead bodies of the two enemies. They had lived in hate of each other and died hating each other, locked together in a final eternal embrace . . .

Erin Cunningham (11)
Northleigh CE Primary School, Malvern

He's Coming

He's coming, I can hear him, he's coming up the stairs. He's looking for me, he knows I'm here. I'm trying to hide from the terror within. It's getting closer and closer, and at any moment it might strike!

'Miaow! . . .' After all that, it's a cat.

Ben Essenhigh (9)
Northleigh CE Primary School, Malvern

The Monster Boy

Late last night I dreamed I turned into a monster. But my mum told me I turned into a creature in real life. So tonight I'm going to see if I change . . .

I have turned into a creature but I can't turn back into a human being, help!

Thomas Howells (9)
Northleigh CE Primary School, Malvern

What A Naughty Cat

Once there lived a girl called Lucy. Lucy lived at boarding school with her best friend Laura. Lucy had blue eyes and brown hair that she usually put in a pony tail. She had a pet parrot called Billy. Laura had brown eyes and blonde curly hair and a cat called Tilly.

It was a Wednesday morning. Lucy and Laura went down to get some breakfast. On the way Tilly tripped up and scared Billy. So he tripped up and knocked down a big picture of Queen Elizabeth 1st. But in its place was a big door. They forgot about breakfast and opened the door. They saw a long path at the end, there was a door there too. So they opened it and to their amazement they saw a lovely garden. There were lovely pink blue and gold flowers.

They sat on a nice bench. 'Oi that's my bench.' They started to run very fast. They went through the door and locked it. When they got to the end they put the picture back up and went to have breakfast!

Annabel Pearson (8)
Northleigh CE Primary School, Malvern

Silverspray's Day

'Hi, I'm Lydia. I've transformed into my Orca, Silverspray. So now I can leap quite high! Now, I'm pretty hungry, so, live fish, coming up! . . . *Crunch!* . . . Not bad. 'Lydia!' My family! They're searching for me! There's a shark about to attack the boat. OK . . . OK. *Bonk!* Oops! I hit him on the nose. Wait, he's gone. Phew!'

(15 minutes Later). *'We need directions to Sydney!'* came a voice. It was a clownfish and a blue fish called Martin, and Dory.They spoke whale to me and said they were looking for Nemo (who?) I helped them out and then I felt a tingle in my body, an urge to rise to the surface, on when I did, I changed back! What a day!

Leah Ashley (9)
Northleigh CE Primary School, Malvern

The Teased Tarantula!

One day in the centre of the zoo there lived a big, hairy, duck-faced, camel-tailed tarantula. She was hairy and nobody in the world would want to be her friend and they never will.

One day she was sitting in the corner of her glass-faced cage and she decided to go and visit her friend next door. Jessica!

'Hi Jessica!' exclaimed Sandy.

'Hi Sandy!' answered Jessica.

'You're my only friend,' said Sandy.

'Well,' Jessica pronounced, 'let's go and find some new friends then.'

'Come on.'

So they hopped out of their cage like they had popped their corks.

On the way round the zoo they bumped into a chimpanzee.

Sandy asked, 'Do you want to be my friend?'

'Who would want to be friends with you?' answered Rebecca the chimpanzee. 'You duck-faced, camel-tailed freak.'

'Oh, oh, well that's it,' Sandy said, heartbroken.

On the way back Sandy and Jessica got surrounded by laughing giraffes, monkeys, zebras, snakes, wolves, elephants, rhinos and hippos. She let out the biggest scream in her whole entire lifetime. 'Aaaaargh!' which burst everyone's eardrums. They never laughed at Sandy that duck-faced camel-tailed freak tarantula again!

Bye!

Holly Kempster (9)
Northleigh CE Primary School, Malvern

Matthew, Jake And James Go Spying

One day a little boy called Jake was walking down the road and he saw his friends Matthew and James. 'Do you want to come quad biking later?'

'Yes!' said Jake. 'We will meet you at the park at 1 o'clock.'

The time went slowly. At last it was 1 o'clock, so they went around the park. James saw something. A smuggler jumped out and Jake, James and Matthew quad-biked home. Then they called the police who caught the bad men and they lived happily ever after.

James Dickens (9)
Northleigh CE Primary School, Malvern

Teddy With The Red Nose

Once there was a teddy, who Bethany loved. She took him everywhere.

One day it was snowing and Bethany decided to take Teddy for a walk. She set off, then when she was halfway there she decided to make a snowman, so she put Teddy down for a minute. When she'd made it she went home without Teddy. Then Teddy saw another teddy. She said, 'Hello.'

Teddy said, 'How did you get here?'

'Somebody forgot me.'

Teddy said, 'Anyway, what's your name?'

'Rosie.'

Teddy said, 'Rosie, why don't you come with me?'

'But you don't know the way.'

'Yes I do, I'll follow the footprints.'

So they set off. In five minutes they got home and then they sat down in the snow. Bethany came outside and grabbed them, but now Teddy had a red nose because it was so cold!

Bethany Burton (9)
Northleigh CE Primary School, Malvern

A Day In The Life Of An Ant

Hi, I'm Anne the ant, ever wondered what it's like to be an ant. Yes, well come with me then.

Yum, time for breakfast (which we have to find ourselves). Hey there's some muffin crumbs on the table, mmm my favourite.

I'm going up the beech tree, come on! Ah, it's nice and shady up here. Oh look the Johnsons are going on a picnic. Let's tell the others. Get in, it's very comfortable dry and soft.

Yum, zzzz. We're here. I must have fallen asleep. That was delicious but it was hard dodging everybody's feet though.

The day's almost over but before tea and bed it's time for dance of the ant. It's like a normal dance only just for ants. I'm having more crumbs for tea.

Time for bed, bye!

Emma Pallen (8)
Northleigh CE Primary School, Malvern

The Tiny Alien

Once upon a time there was a tiny alien called Zloggy. One day he was fixing his ship the Glozzle 11. It had crashed into a tree. Suddenly someone started his rocket while he was inside! His rocket wasn't properly fixed so it went haywire and he zoomed off to Earth.

He landed with a *bump* and shook his head. Then from the top of the mountain of little bumpy things (stairs) came a huge monster wearing a blue T-shirt and green shorts. It was a fierce Declan monster! He ran as fast as he could but he scooped Xloggy up and took him to his cave, or in other words bedroom.

Anyway Declan wasn't a monster and decided to teach Zloggy that his room wasn't a cave and the stairs weren't mountains. So now Declan and Xloggy are best friends.

Declan Amphlett (8)
Northleigh CE Primary School, Malvern

A Dragon Called Nick

There once was a dragon called Nick and nobody wanted to be his friend. Well it wasn't exactly that, but he couldn't have any friends because nobody lived anywhere near him.

One day Nick went out for a picnic on his favourite hill. Nick had named it 'Picnic Peak' because it was the perfect place for a picnic. Nick picnicked every week but this week he was upon Picnic Peak when he heard wailing. Nick was so surprised that he floated up a bit with his wings.

Nick went down to investigate, he took his little picnic basket in case he needed it. What Nick found was a little boy, he asked the boy what had happened.

The boy answered, 'Who are you?' in an innocent voice.

'I'm a dragon,' answered Nick politely.

'Eek!' shouted the boy. 'Please don't hurt me. I haven't done anything wrong,' cried the boy.

'Dear little boy, I wouldn't want to hurt you. I know, why don't you come back to my cave?' asked Nick sweetly.

'I would love to,' murmured the boy in an unsure voice.

So Nick and the little boy went back to Nick's cave. At Nick's cave, Nick asked, 'Now please tell me what happened.'

The boy couldn't really remember but they exchanged stories. After that the boy very slowly said, 'Please could I . . . live . . . here?'

'Of course you can.' And they lived happily every after. Nick having given a friend, the boy, a home.

Jamie Mackenzie (9)
Northleigh CE Primary School, Malvern

A Day In The Life Of Michel

I got up from my lovely sleep and found myself on a deserted island surrounded by a shroud of mist. I found a lush green forest, but while thumping through the forest I couldn't see but I knew I was being watched by one hundred staring eyes. I was being followed by something, but what?

Me and my dog Stella, found a small hill. I watched all around me for a ship but there was too much mist around me. I felt isolated but somehow not alone. I decided to light a fire to stop the bitter cold of the night, and keep those murderous mosquitoes off my skin.

When I'd lit the fire it started to go out so I went to get more firewood, but when I got back there was a very strange man scooping sand over my fire. Then he said in a low tone, 'No fire!' Then he drew a long line in the sand and said, 'This my end, that yours across the domain also no swim.'

I was so enraged by this but I kept my mood in check.

One day I was so enraged by this I made a huge beacon of wood and then when I lit the fire I saw him - he stamped out the fire. I was angry then I was going to swim in the sea and that's what I did. I paddled for all I was worth, but then I felt a searing pain run down my back, then I saw a huge jellyfish poised for the kill. I knew I was dead.

Joe Woolcott (11)
Northleigh CE Primary School, Malvern

The Golden Goal

Hi, I'm Charlie and I love football, so I joined a football club where David Beckham came in for three days in two weeks. I waited, waited and waited. The long day came and it went well until Andy Grenn sprained my ankle! It is true, I was in hospital and it hurt, it hurt more when I was told I was out for eight days.

I was home two days later. My dad rang the club to say I'd be back on match day. When my friend Joe came round we had a little kick around. Joe was a great goalie and he really helped me with my shots.

'So what happened with Andy?' Joe asked.

'Two footed slide,' I answered.

'Ouch,' said Joe.

I agreed.

The day before the match some of my team's rivals came round and said bad things about me.

The next day my dad took me. We were 1-0 down at half-time. Aron scored 2, I came on in goal and Josh Plupsted gave a penalty in stoppage time. Troy, the top scorer, came to hit the ball to the left all the way into my hands, then the ref blew the whistle, and that's how to stop a golden goal!

Charlie Bytheway (9)
Northleigh CE Primary School, Malvern

The Day Hamish Escaped

It was about a week ago now and I'm still mad at Megan for letting him out.

It was Monday afternoon and I was coming home from school. I got home and naturally ran to my bedroom (we live in a bungalow, so there's no stairs to climb up). Anyway, I was just about to open Hamish's cage door when I saw it was already open. My first thought was that Megan, my annoying little show-off three-year-old sister, had stolen him to show to Katie our babysitter. So I stormed into Megan's room all set to lecture her on how to hold Hamish properly when I found her on her bed reading her Milly Molly Mandy book. 'Um Megan,' I said startled, 'where's Hamish?'

'Mum's room,' she answered very quickly.

I ran to Mum's room, Hamish was on the bed. I jumped on and screamed, 'Got ya.' As I screamed I clasped my hands round his furry body. 'Oh Hamish, if Megan let you out she will pay!' I said and put him in his cage.

Frankie Shackleton (9)
Northleigh CE Primary School, Malvern

Doe The Daredevil

One day there lived a boy called Doe who was a daredevil. He tried very dangerous stunts, once he jumped out of his bedroom window and broke his leg.

Doe lived in a town where a superhero lived and a villain lived.

One day he did a stunt that nearly killed him, he was planning to unicycle over a boiling lake of lava, everybody was watching him. When he was nearly at the end evil Eric pushed him off!

Going, going . . . just in time Superhero Sam rescued him!

Joe Brooker (9)
Northleigh CE Primary School, Malvern

The Crow That Couldn't Call

There was once a young crow, who at first couldn't call. All the other animals and his family had a try, but only one succeeded. I'll tell you what happened . . .

It was early in the morning, and all the animals were waking up. All the crows were out hunting for their breakfast. They all caught something, but after breakfast all the animals had a plan to frighten the youngest crow, Albert. It was so that if he was in danger, they knew that he would call for help.

Albert had just finished his breakfast, when suddenly he heard a loud growl from underneath him. The little bird looked down from the branch and saw it was just Cat. 'Hello Cat! Out for a morning stroll?' said Albert in a cheerful voice.

'Hi,' said Cat as he went back indoors.

But just then a sawing noise came from underneath him. It was Dog, he was pretending to saw down the tree.

'Hi Dog!' said Albert as Dog ran inside.

But then, just as he was going into the nest he heard his sister calling for help, he knew he couldn't help her so he called for help too. And that's how Albert learned to call.

Kate Richards (9)
Northleigh CE Primary School, Malvern

My Strange Week

Dear Diary,

Sorry I haven't written in you for ages, I have had my own problems. I couldn't write and I was very busy. I'll tell you about it.

Well last Monday I woke up and found my house had grown. I got out of bed and my younger sister came out of her bedroom and jumped at the sight of me rushing past and she nearly stepped on me! She called, 'Dad, there's a mouse in the house,' and my dad quickly jumped out of bed and started setting up the mousetraps. Mum was just going outside to water the plants and I quickly scuttled outside. I wondered where to go. Luckily I remembered there was a pet shop round the corner.

A giant hand wrapped around me, I got put in a box thing with some dry stuff. In my box there was a circle thing with a space on the inside, I stepped inside . . . I started to walk then run, I thought I was getting somewhere but I was staying in the same place then I went to explore my bed.

A couple of days later I was taken out of my box and put in another one. It went dark and I felt it moving. I could hear talking, it sounded a bit like this:

'Name.'
'Call Max.'
'No!'
'Call Whiskers.'
'Stupid name.'
'Name Pouchy.'
'Yes Pouchy.'

I realised I was back home! And my little sister Jasmine was my owner. Oh no!

Gemma James (9)
Northleigh CE Primary School, Malvern

The Giant's Version Of Jack And The Beanstalk

All I know is I was eating my breakfast when this boy came and stole my chickens, so what I did was . . . I ran towards him. When Jack saw me he let one of the chickens go. I said, 'Are you hungry?' Then he chopped my beanstalk down. 'Ow, ow!'

Isabel Massey (9)
Northleigh CE Primary School, Malvern

A Day In The Brownies

One day, on a Saturday, I went to the woods with the Brownies. When we were there a man cut down huge trees and we made a den out of it. After that we had our lovely packed lunches from home. A few minutes later we played 'duck, duck, goose'. That was fun, even though I wasn't the goose.

It was getting near night-time so we got some twigs and made a big pile out of them. The man got some matches and lit them up and then we had marshmallows. (They're lovely when you put them over the fire and you eat them burnt!)

Ellie Cornelius (8)
Northleigh CE Primary School, Malvern

It Seemed Very Deep

The water seemed very cruel. It was freezing! I thought I was going to die, but then I forgot I can't swim. I was terrified, I needed my mum. My mum gave me a towel and said, 'Get out!' Then I saw I was only in the bath. How extremely stupid.

Hannah Rodwell (10)
Willows Primary School, Lichfield

The Computer Game

I tried and tried to kill the invaders. I pressed the wrong key and I zoomed to a different planet! It felt strange because I was sitting at home all alone on my computer. I had two minutes left before the game ended. The clock ticked . . . my time was over!

Kayleigh Wincup (10)
Willows Primary School, Lichfield

Earthquake!

My legs were shaking. I'd got the impression I was going to fall. There was some music. I thought it was an earthquake! My heart was beating hard and my sister was feeling the same! I was scared, but happy at the same time as we were just dancing madly!

Sophie Hoggarth (10)
Willows Primary School, Lichfield

The Dragon

I ran as I was followed by a fierce, terrifying dragon. It was as fast as ten sports cars and I was not even the speed of one. Its burning fire scorched tree after tree until eventually I managed to escape and hide. I was panting, worn out but relieved.

Tommy Ratcliffe (9)
Willows Primary School, Lichfield

The Dream

I splashed people as quickly as I could, trying to be like someone famous. I thought it was real. I woke up, it was only a dream. It was time to get my school clothes on. I went downstairs for breakfast and rushed to the high school in town.

Nicole Bradley (10)
Willows Primary School, Lichfield

Drowning

I can't swim! I'm petrified of icy cold water. Then all of a sudden, I felt bubbles floating out of my mouth. My nose was blocked and water poured over my face. It was then I realised I was standing under a freezing cold, soaking wet hanging basket getting soaked!

Samantha Bicknell (10)
Willows Primary School, Lichfield

It's Coming!

As my claw shivered, I walked closer and . . . argh! I saw this giant five-fingered monster coming down at me. It picked me up off the floor then it placed me in the gloomy cage. Once I was in I realised that it was the person that looks after me.

Lucy Jones (9)
Willows Primary School, Lichfield

The Fast And The Furious

My legs were shaking in fright. My head was thundering madly. I was so scared I was going to crash. I trembled in fear as suddenly we screeched to a shuddering stop. My mind whizzed! I smiled in relief. I jumped out of the busy roller coaster and laughed excitedly.

Kerry-Anne Jessop (10)
Willows Primary School, Lichfield

The Alien Invasion

I froze still as the murky, monster crept forward. I shot swiftly as the slimy thing surprised me. My heart was pumping crazily. I screamed loudly and then my annoying Mum turned the nail-biting PlayStation off. It was bath time and the end of my frightening and brilliant adventure.

Kirsty Ashley (10)
Willows Primary School, Lichfield

Tasty

Once I was making jam tarts and I was going to eat them. Suddenly, it spat at me and looked at me like a ghost. I squeaked like a mouse, running as fast as I could and I hid under my bed. I looked again, but it was not real!

Stephen Wilkins (10)
Willows Primary School, Lichfield

Don't Eat Me!

One day I was fishing and caught a fish. It was 7cm wide and 16cm long. Suddenly it gobbled me in one gulp!

Inside the fish it was disgusting. It was like a giant whale cut open. Well, it went crazy and spat me out and I swam away wildly.

Luke Sheldon (10)
Willows Primary School, Lichfield

Race Driver

I was going down to the shop and I was going home and I saw a Ferrari F50. I jumped in, shot off at a hundred miles an hour. My heart was racing and I felt nervous. Suddenly, I crashed into a lamp post.

The game was over.

Robert Rhodes (10)
Willows Primary School, Lichfield

The Missile At War!

They stand in line like soldiers waiting for the signal. The missile heading towards them at great speed, eagerly awaiting, hoping to defend the honour. Using their bodies like shields, they deflect the offending weapon into the distance. The whistle blows, the war is over, we are the cup winners!

Jamie Lees (10)
Willows Primary School, Lichfield

Ratty

Jamie Lees was in bed and fell fast asleep with his rat. Something ran across his face. Jamie jumped in a terrible panic, because he has a fear of spiders, he automatically thought it was a spider. In the end it was his lovely pet rat in bed with him!

Gary Brown (10)
Willows Primary School, Lichfield

It's A Ghost!

I was walking down to the shops. Suddenly something scary was chasing me saying, *'Kill!'*

I started running as fast as I could but he was still behind me. I couldn't find anywhere to hide so I ran as fast as I could down the alley, him still following me . . .

Steven Bayliss (10)
Willows Primary School, Lichfield

The Shakes

My hands were shaking. I had butterflies in my belly. My legs were shivering. I was getting nervous. I had to go through the door. My heart was beating as fast as it could. I was hot and bothered as well. I'm so daft being terrified about our school play!

Rebecca Johnson-Tiso (10)
Willows Primary School, Lichfield

Robot Wars

I was running wildly around, not very fast, laughing because I was made of metal. Someone was trying to shoot me. I rapidly transformed into a jet and I blew him up with a rocket. There was a big bang and suddenly the screen flashed madly saying, 'Game over!'

David Smallman (10)
Willows Primary School, Lichfield

The Shadows

Slowly I slid into the freezing, deep, cold water. Dark shadows surrounded me. I had nowhere to go. Not moving a muscle, frozen like an ice cube. Afraid to breathe, eyes darting in every direction. Closer, closer, they came as if sniffing me. As quickly as they came, they vanished!

Daniel Jewell (9)
Willows Primary School, Lichfield

The Speedy Car

Nervously, I jumped into the car. Suddenly it started to pick up speed. I clung onto the wheel, knowing if I let go, I would spin! I slammed the brake as hard as I could. *Screech!* It stopped still. I nagged Mum for money to go on the ride again!

Aston Blackwell (10)
Willows Primary School, Lichfield

The Night Creeper

I woke with a start, with my toes all exposed, sweating. Suddenly an enormous shadow monster leapt out and started creeping across the landing. It started to grow monstrously! I whispered silently, 'Who's there?' and flicked on the light. Relief! It was only my clothes on the chair!

Alex Foyle (10)
Willows Primary School, Lichfield

Up In The Clouds

My hands are trembling. My legs are like jelly. My toes are sweating like it's raining. My stomach is turning inside out as if it were empty. My arms are as loose as string, blowing in the wind.

'Come on mate,' encouraged Josh, 'you're at the top of the ladder!'

James Meakin (9)
Willows Primary School, Lichfield

The School Bus

Everyone pushed onto the bus. They zoomed out of the gate. Off they went in the bus on the trip. They started to chat noisily apart from Lucy. Lucy could not wait to get there. Everyone waved happily to their parents. Then Lucy moaned loudly. 'Are we nearly there yet?'

Rachel Wood (10)
Willows Primary School, Lichfield

Terrifying Tyrannosaurus-Rex

There he was! I came face to face with a huge Tyrannosaurus-Rex! He stared at me. I fought ferociously through the lush green grass. His sharp, scaly claws dodged me. He was going to eat me . . . alive!

Mrs Joint nudged me from my nightmare. 'Stop daydreaming and get on!'

Megan Shenton (10)
Willows Primary School, Lichfield

A Mile To Go In The Swimming Pool

My arms sprung forward, as I swam quickly. With my legs kicking, I flew forward. This was going to be my only chance to win. I felt excited and my heart pounded nervously. It would be my best time yet. 'Nearly there!' I spluttered as I reached the bath taps.

Michelle Wilcox (10)
Willows Primary School, Lichfield

Don't Let It Near Me!

My legs were wobbling like mad. I had fear all the way through me. 'I can't do it! I can't go near it. Someone help!' My hands trembled swiftly. I didn't want to see the fierce, ugly tarantula.

'It won't harm you,' laughed Mum, 'it's only an ant!'

Thomas McCaffrey (10)
Willows Primary School, Lichfield

It's A Miracle!

The lush thick grass swayed as it rushed past me. Thunderous roars filled the air as suddenly it pounced. I jumped in fright! Monstrous screams flew back as it hurtled towards me! I took one speedy step back and blasted the ball right past the distraught goalie.

Ryan Poxon (10)
Willows Primary School, Lichfield

Falling

My hands started to shake hesitantly and my legs began to shiver briskly. I was falling. *Help!* It was my worst nightmare. Miserably and madly I screeched anxiously again. *Help!*

As I started to reach the safe and stable land, I decided I'd never go in an aeroplane ever again.

Polly Bourne (10)
Willows Primary School, Lichfield

The Big Race!

I was off to a zooming start. I rapidly raced down the track leaving a track of fire behind. Wildly I sprinted hastily. With my eyes bulging, I knocked the racer out the way. I had nearly finished. The snail race had finished. Stubbornly I walked home. My best yet 10cm!

George Makin (10)
Willows Primary School, Lichfield

Trying To Escape From A Dinosaur!

Gary's hands were sweating with fear. Anxiety was creeping down his spine. Gary was trying his hardest to climb to the top. He spotted a beast and squealed. Gary's mouth tightened. It crawled onto his hand. He pushed up for his last stretch, reaching the top of the bunk bed!

Ben Cunningham (10)
Willows Primary School, Lichfield

Die Another Day!

My legs trembled. I hated the noise. Blades blasted forward. Luckily, I escaped. My body grew tighter. Closer it came! I zoomed. I didn't want to lose another life. I managed the biggest hiss I've ever done. My pace lowered. So close! That frightening lawnmower better not come out again!

Maria Sammons (10)
Willows Primary School, Lichfield

Attacked!

I swam frantically, away from it. I kept rushing towards the edge, trying to hide from it, but it kept finding me and chasing round and round until I couldn't take it anymore.

When I grabbed the side, I wailed, 'Why have I got to go swimming with my brother?'

Sean Wood (9)
Willows Primary School, Lichfield

When I Stepped Out Into The Night!

Her heart was beating and trembling quickly. She was there rapidly, her arms and legs were shaking as the wind was flying through her face. Thinking she was going to crash, she was sweating terribly. As she stepped into the night, she knew she was about to be in trouble . . .

Sophie Davies (9)
Willows Primary School, Lichfield

The Lush Green Jungle

I was tearing through lush leaves. I couldn't escape from the drowning water. My freezing legs shivered. 'Help!' I cried, but no one was there. This was the end! I scrambled away from the huge jungle. At last it was over. 'Hooray!' I shouted. 'They've finally turned off that dreadful sprinkler.'

Hannah Frazer-Morris (10)
Willows Primary School, Lichfield